She wanted to say something to tell him how lovely everything looked. How he'd done a wonderful job with his house and furnishings. She turned to tell him, but his gaze stopped her. His look seared her soul with desire and beckoned her toward him. As if she traveled through time and space, she found his embrace.

Daniel held her close and rested his chin on the top of her head. "I don't know how we found each other, but I'm glad we did." He turned her face up and claimed her lips.

The fiery kiss stirred a passion that bloomed in her belly and raced through her blood. He stopped kissing her and she inhaled a deep breath. The smell of leather and everything Daniel fanned the flames. She wanted this man and he wanted her. She closed her eyes and bit her bottom lip. Would he think she an immoral woman if she let him love her?

He put his fingers under her chin and tugged her face up. "Are you all right?"

The tenderness she found in his eyes answered her question. "I am." She placed her hands around his neck and pulled his face to hers. She kissed him, opening her mouth to his sensual kiss. She followed his lead as he waltzed her around the room. He held her close while his fingers gently caressed her body, and his mouth did wonderful things to her lips.

Previous Releases by Jane Lewis

LOVE AT FIVE THOUSAND FEET
THE BARNSTORMER
THE LADY FLYER

Home in Wylder

by

Jane Lewis

The Wylder West

Home in Wylder

Cover Art by *Tina Lynn Stout*

The Wild Rose Press, Inc.
PO Box 708
Adams Basin, NY 14410-0708
Visit us at www.thewildrosepress.com

Publishing History
First Edition, 2021
Trade Paperback ISBN 978-1-5092-3537-7
Digital ISBN 978-1-5092-3538-4

The Wylder West
Published in the United States of America

Dedication

For Kim and the many hours of laughter and fun
you bring to this writing journey,
but most of all the privilege to call you friend.

Chapter One

Wylder, Wyoming
August 1878

A train whistle and the screeching of brakes ended the long journey from Georgia to Wyoming. Sarah Miller held to her seat as she lurched forward and then back. It was done, she'd arrived in Wylder. She sat still as a mouse not wanting to be found when the Pullman Porter approached. "Time to disembark, ma'am. Other people's a-waitin' to board."

She acknowledged his kindness with a smile. "Thank you, Emmanuel, you've been very gracious." Her legs wobbled as she rose from her seat and she clutched the conductor's arm to regain her balance. He steadied her, his touch soothing a bit of her fear. "Will you arrange for my trunk to be taken to Lowery's Dress Shoppe?"

"Sure will. Best of luck to ya." He tipped his hat.

"Thank you, I don't think I would have made it this far without you." She stood straight as the mantra they recited at the start of each class at the finishing school echoed in her mind. Stand straight, walk with your head high, be considerate, and don't let your suitors think you know more than they do. The first three were ingrained to memory but the fourth command left her angry. "I will not act like a dunce," she whispered

1

under her breath as she departed the railcar.

She cemented herself to the platform as people swarmed around with their bags and children underfoot. The directions to her aunt's dress shop rested in her trunk. What did the instructions say? Never mind—they would come. She strolled past the depot office and into the street. A man on horseback tipped his hat and smiled. She dipped her head and gave him a slight grin before she crossed the street and walked toward a tall building. Two men herded cattle down the middle of the street.

A lace handkerchief held to her nose did nothing to keep the dust and smell of cow dung from penetrating her nostrils. She stood close to a building, turned her face away and waited for them to pass. She coughed and brushed dust from her dress. The town bustled with men on horseback, in wagons and walking in and out of buildings. Someone loaded feed sacks into the back of a wagon. Sarah did a double look when she realized it was a woman in denim pants and a straw hat. Another lady in a skirt with a bodice barely keeping her bosom contained hurried into the tall building.

Maybe she entered the dress shop for a fitting with Aunt Mildred. As she walked toward the structure two men approached her.

"Hello, can you help me?" As soon as the words left her mouth, she wanted to take them back. "Never mind, sorry to bother you." She pressed her elbows close to her side to make her body small enough to fit through the space between the wall and the man.

Her leg muscles tensed, ready to run, until both men thwarted her escape as if she were a ball in a keep-away game. Fear turned to anger as they corralled her like a wild horse. The younger man laughed and revealed a lack of several front teeth as his sour breath blew over her face. She fought the need to retch and the spasm hurled her shoulders forward. A gasp of air entered her lungs, she cleared her throat and swallowed the bile. "Please excuse me. I thought you were someone else. Now, if you'll let me be on my way." An old drunk staggered past them and brushed against her. Sarah took the opportunity and jerked to the right; her legs poised to run.

The leader grabbed her arm. "We ain't through with you, little lady." He pulled her close and raked her from face to her breasts. "Bet you've never been with a real man a'fore." He addressed the other man. "What do you think, Silus?"

"Never seen such a fancy girl." Silus patted her bustle. We'll have fun with her, won't we, Jasper?"

The man rubbed his other hand down the front of her dress lingering on her breasts. "You sho' is temptin', how 'bout we have a little fun?"

Sarah tugged, but his grip dug into her arm like a vise. Her hand grew numb from lack of circulation. The street surged with crowds of people who went about their business as if this were an everyday occurrence. A kick to the man's shin with her velvet boot prompted an evil laugh from him, blinding pain to her toes, and knocked her off-balance. He jerked her closer; she attempted to bring her knee to his groin, but the fancy dress prevented the assault. His strong hold jerked her toward him, and her hat tumbled to the ground causing her tresses to escape the pins.

Jasper held her body against his and assaulted her mouth with a brutal kiss. Her scalp burned as he

3

wrenched his hold on her hair. She twisted her head, opened her mouth, and yelled, "Help!"

A large fist clipped her abductor's jaw, his body slammed into hers and she staggered against the wall of the building. A scream filled the air, she put her hand over her mouth when she realized the sound had come from her. Her rescuer fought both men and was winning until the man with the missing teeth regained his footing and grabbed the good Samaritan's hands and held them behind his back. Just as Jasper readied his fist, the telltale click of a rifle being cocked split the air. A huge red-haired man pointed the rifle toward the fight. Lord in heaven, would this ever end? Whose side was he on? She walked sideways with her back to the wall and planned her escape until she heard his command.

"Keep it up and I'll kill the both of ye." The giant walked forward. Sarah bent at the waist and sucked air into her lungs. Her rescuer leaned against a post and the man with the Scottish brogue kept his rifle pointed at her captors.

The two men grabbed their hats. The leader said, "I'll catch you one day without the rifle and I'll blow your head off."

The Scotsman pointed the rifle in the air and fired. "That day's not today."

Sarah jumped at the sound of the gunshot and fell against the wall, her legs barely able to hold her body upright.

"You son of a bitch, foreigner." Jasper puffed his chest out. "You ain't welcome in this town. And as for you, pretty boy," he addressed the man who interrupted his tryst with the girl, "Daniel Taylor, you ain't as smart as you think you are. I'll take care of your ass, too."

"I'll take you one-on-one any day and we'll see who wins." Daniel stood to his full height still rubbing his belly.

Her attackers shuffled backward until they reached the end of the building, then turned and headed down the street.

She prayed the wall would envelop her and she would reappear in her bedroom at home. She closed her eyes and forbade herself to cry.

The long-haired bearded man who first came to her aid picked up her hat and knocked the dust off. "I'm sorry, ma'am. They had no right to accost you. Name's Daniel Taylor and this is my friend Callum MacPhilip. What's a proper lady like you doing on this street?"

She took her hat and gazed into the brown eyes of a handsome man who appeared to be around her age if not a few years older. Long hair to his shoulders matched the color of the sprinkling of hair on his chest escaping the rip in his shirt. The gaping hole flapped open and a rippling of muscle showed as he kneeled and picked up her gold hairpin. Her heart hammered in her chest. She fought the urge to fall in his arms and weep. As if he recognized her thoughts, he and his friend stepped back and gave her space. She gathered her hair and secured it before she placed her hat on her head and tied the ribbon.

Daniel collected his Stetson from the street and held it in his hands. "Glad we were in town to assist."

Where were her manners? "Of course, I'm so sorry this happened. I don't know what they would have done if you hadn't come along."

"Good thing you fought back." He nodded toward

his friend. "Gave Callum time to grab his rifle."

She adjusted her gloves. "Where I'm from, this doesn't happen."

"And where's that?" He brushed dirt off his pants.

"I'm from Savannah, Georgia." She straightened her spine and talked faster, she had to get to her aunt's dress shop or wait for the next train back home. "I came here to see my aunt. She owns Lowery's Dress Shoppe. Do you know where her store's located? I must get there before anything else happens." These men appeared amiable, but she didn't know them either. James had been nice, too. Look where that got her. Here.

"I know where the Widow Lowery's shop is. If you don't mind, we'll escort you there, make sure Jasper and Silus Nelson don't try to attack you again." He stepped back and let her walk ahead of them.

Jasper and Silus Nelson. She memorized the names and placed their faces in her memory. These men she would avoid at all costs. "Are they brothers?"

"They are." Daniel responded. "Best to keep as far away from them as possible."

"I plan to do just that." She glanced back at the men. "It was a long train ride from Georgia." She didn't know how to make small talk to cowboys and hoped she didn't sound silly.

"I'm sure it was, you must be tired." Daniel nodded toward the next street. "Go straight, turn right and the shop is on the left. It's an easy town to figure out but unless you need a horse at the Livery, want to go to the Saloon, or heading out of town on the train, I'd say stay off Old Cheyenne Road."

She turned the corner and spotted the sign,

Lowery's Dress Shoppe. *Oh, thank God.* She closed her eyes and said a prayer.

He opened the door to the establishment and stepped aside. "Delivered safe and sound. Good luck to you and remember keep to the safe side of town if you're unaccompanied."

She stared at the two men. "Thank you, Daniel and Callum. I'll not forget your kindness." She also reminded herself the men's names were Daniel Taylor and Callum MacPhilip. The older man had red hair and he was a large muscular man with a chiseled jaw and handsome face, but the younger man had her swooning and forgetting she'd ever met James. This would be a story to relate to her friends when she returned to Savannah.

She entered the store. Bolts of fabric and thread lined the walls. A blue velvet caught her eye and she pulled off her glove and ran her fingers over the fabric.

"If'n you're partial to the velvet, I'll give you a good price." Mildred Lowery approached her.

"Aunt Mildred." She ran to her aunt and put her arms around the old woman.

The woman stepped back. "I ain't no hugger. You must be Sarah. Winnie said she was sendin' a picture but never did." She sized up her niece. "A slip of a thing, you are, but we'll find you work somewhere."

"Work?" She couldn't imagine ever leaving this store after her encounter with the bad men. "Mama said I would work in your shop, sewing and embroidering."

"Embroidering?" Mildred cackled. "Ain't many women in this town interested in fancy embroidery excepting maybe the whores. They got to look good for their gentlemen, you know. 'Sides, I got a seamstress, can't afford to pay two."

"Whores? What kind of town is this?" Sarah found a chair and sat.

"This is the west, Missy. I told your uppity Ma you shouldn't come but she said you insisted and frankly they were tired of the scandal."

Sarah removed her hat and placed it on a table with her gloves. "I didn't know Mother told you. I made a stupid mistake." This wasn't the way she expected her first meeting with her mother's sister to go.

Mildred handed her a piece of paper. "Here's the rules, wrote 'em down so you'd have 'em. You can live here. I've got a room upstairs I'll rent ya. You have to get a job and pay me board every week. No men in the store or your room and no running around town getting yourself into trouble. This is a rough place, and some people would just as soon kill you as to look at you."

Her aunt was so different from her mother, she wondered how they came out of the same womb. Winifred was refined and polite where this woman was rude and downright mean. "I'll follow the rules, Aunt Mildred." After her encounter with Jasper and Silus she understood what could happen.

Mildred crossed her arms and stared at her niece. "Everyone calls me Widow Lowery, that goes for you, too. They just brought your trunk, I'll show you your room and tomorrow, we'll find you a position."

She followed her aunt outside and up the stairs. A whistle sounded, she turned to see Jasper and Silus leaning against a post watching her. She grabbed her aunt's arm and steadied her shaking legs.

Mildred nodded toward the men. "Those two are the perfect example of what's wrong in this town. Stay away from the likes of them."

Sarah kept the tremble out of her voice. "Does this room have a lock for the door?"

Her aunt pulled the key from her pocket and placed it in the keyhole. "Yes, Missy, and those heathens know better than to come around, I've chased them off enough."

Sarah's nerves settled but she sure didn't trust those men. How many like them, or worse, lived in this town? She stepped into the sparse room with a small bed, table with a pitcher and bowl, one chair and her trunk.

Widow Lowery studied her. "I know this ain't what you're used to but it's how it is in Wylder. Take it or find a room at the boarding house."

She opened her trunk. "I'll take it and I'm grateful, Aunt... I mean Widow Lowery."

Mildred pulled some dresses from the trunk. "These fancy clothes are as useless as settin' a milk bucket under a bull. I told your ma to send some plain dresses for you to work in. You might get by with some of this for Sunday church but careful you don't go 'round lookin' like a whore or saloon girl."

Sarah pulled out a brown dress from the bottom of the pile. "I brought this. Will it do?" She wouldn't admit she defied her mother and brought her best except for this ugly frock.

The old woman examined the material. "Fine, let me see what shoes you got on."

She lifted her dress and displayed her black velvet boots.

"Might as well sell them to a harlot." Mildred laughed. "What with the dust and the rain and snow 'round here they'll get ruined quick."

She pulled out a pair of black leather boots. "I brought these."

Mildred examined the heel of the shoes. "These'll do if you ain't standin' in 'em all day. When you get some money ahead, I'll sell you suitable cloth and you can make another dress in your spare time. Two ought to be enough until winter comes. Gets real cold in these parts, better save money for a warm coat, too."

She'd be home by winter, that was for sure. Sarah searched through the trunk for her money bag. "I need to send a telegram to Mother and let her know I arrived."

"Telegraph office is open now. I'll send it for you. One dollar, please." She held out her hand.

Sarah passed two half dollars to her aunt. "Thank you."

The old woman grabbed the coins. "While you've got your money out, might as well pay for your board. I'm charging you two dollars a week."

Sarah withdrew silver dollars from the bag and handed it over. Her coin was disappearing fast. She had her money for the return trip to Savannah sewn into the lining of her trunk. That was her secret, not anything she would share with the old lady.

"Much obliged. Better search for some work on the morrow." Mildred placed the coins in her pocket. "I'll bring you up something to eat tonight. I don't offer maid service or meals, plenty of places to eat in Wylder. Everybody in this town makes their own way."

"Thank you, Widow Lowery." Sarah turned the key as soon as her aunt left and glanced out the window. The bad men stood against the post and stared.

She placed the chair under the doorknob and unpacked her trunk. A turquoise satin dress rested on top of the heap. The excitement of the adventure out west spurred her to bring her best clothes. The hasty decision to flee her home left her no time to investigate just what she would face. If her mother knew, would she have let her come? Maybe she did and wanted to get rid of her so as not to lose her social standing.

Papa appeared sad as she boarded the train; he'd given her a weak wave and trudged away with Mother. Neither of them glanced back. She'd stay until Mama wired and told her to return. Never again would she take her home and her safety for granted.

A gun shot sounded and she jumped off the bed and crouched on the floor. Yells and laughter filled the hot afternoon air. When at last she gathered the courage to peek out the window, she spied a man weaving his way down the middle of the street with a gun in his hand. He appeared intoxicated. Another man approached him and took his gun, then led him to the saloon next door. She returned to the bed and lay on her side with her knees tucked up to her arms. Her body trembled and tears flowed down her cheeks. Why didn't she stay home? She knew the answer and that's what broke her heart. The last words her mother said to her echoed in her mind. "You reap what you sow, girl."

She longed to run down the stairs to find her aunt but was afraid someone would shoot her.

Chapter Two

Card games went on around Daniel and Callum as they sat at a window table in the Five Star Saloon. A piano player tinkled the keys with Camptown Races. Someone bellowed, "Play something else."

Sonny Cash placed a bottle and two glasses on the table. "First one's on me for rescuing the fancy girl from the Nelson brothers. Who was she anyway?"

"Thanks." Daniel poured whiskey in the glasses. "Says she's from Georgia, Widow Lowery's niece."

"No kidding. Never knew the old woman had family."

"Didnae ken, either." Callum knocked back the fire water and picked up the bottle. "Those two scoundrels are gonna kill somebody. Sheriff Hanson needs tae do his job and run them oot of town noo."

"Well, probably ain't gonna happen, as he's just bidin' his time 'til he retires." Sonny ventured back behind the bar.

"Don't drink too much rotten hooch, we still have work at the ranch." Daniel knocked his second drink down and set the glass aside.

"This isn't scotch whiskey, but it'll do. I drank stronger spirits than this when I was a wee boy." He stared into his glass. "Anyway, ye keep all yer Kentucky Whiskey to yourself. I ken you got a supply hid."

"I'm surprised it made the trip in my wagon. I'm surprised we made the trip." He scanned the room.

Callum reflected. "I've made two long voyages in me life, the ship from Scotland to the States and the trip with you to Wyoming. Ye either make it or die and we made it. Lots of death on the way, though. Ever think about going back to Kentucky?"

A saloon girl stood at the table next to them. She put her hand on a gambler's shoulder and gave Daniel a seductive smile. "Every damn day. Every January first I say to myself, I'm giving it one more year." He nodded at the woman and gave her a slight grin.

Callum studied his friend. "No, yer happy in the west. Now, if ye and the bonnie lass get together."

"What bonnie lass are you referring to?" He glanced at the woman again. Hard years at the saloon had stolen her youth. "There aren't any in this town."

"Weren't until today." He poured another drink in Daniel's glass.

"You talking about Sarah Miller?" He threw back the liquid and swallowed. "You fill this glass again and you're drinking it."

"You remember her name. Sarah means princess. Aye, fitting name for the lass, don't ye think?" He eyed his friend over his glass.

Daniel pulled out money and placed it on the table. "What I think is Miss Miller will be taking the next train back to where she came from. Ladies such as her don't stay in this town. They didn't name this place Wylder for nothing."

"Ye don't know what her kind is. Get to ken her, you may be surprised what ye'll find." Callum placed coins on the table.

"You think she's so bonnie, you get to know her. You could save the money you spend at the Wylder Social Club." He made his way out of the saloon.

"Clerty, Clerty, I ken if you went to the Social Club occasionally you wouldn't be such a pain in me bahooky." Callum followed close with his rifle.

Daniel paused and searched the street for the Nelson brothers. Next time he came to town, he'd wear his holster and six-gun. He hoped the girl hadn't ventured out on her own, but disappointment of not seeing her walk along the street filtered through his mind. "Well, you keep going there and you're gonna catch something you can't get rid of." They climbed in the wagon laden with supplies for the week. Daniel collected the leads and guided the team through Sidewinder Lane before taking a right on Wylder Street. He glanced at the dress shop.

Callum chuckled. "Not interested?"

"Whoa." Daniel slowed the horses for the right turn. "What are you talking about, Red?"

"Your head turned completely around when you rode by the dress shop, hoping ye'd get a glimpse of the lass. Besides, you only call me Red if I call you out on something and ye be takin' the long way home. Quicker down Old Cheyenne Road."

He urged the animals to a faster trot as they rode out of town. "I call you Red because my father gave you the nickname. He said your thick red hair drew the ladies and your blazing temper would be the death of you."

Callum stopped talking and Daniel reflected on the day. He'd not seen a woman as pretty as Sarah since he left Lexington, Kentucky five years before. Becca still haunted his dreams and he wondered how she looked now. Was she still as beautiful? She'd married but he had no idea if she had children. He courted two women in Wylder, but they were passing through, didn't take to the climate or hard work. He met a girl just after he arrived who stayed three months and headed to Oregon. Two years later, he met a fine lady who moved to California leaving only a note. He couldn't even remember their names. He stayed away from the Social Club and used hard work to allay his desire. Working from sunup to sundown every damn day left little time to think about such extravagances as a pretty woman.

At the familiar sight of a stand of pines at the edge of his property, he pulled on the leads to slow the wagon. He turned onto his drive and they continued along the spruce-lined lane. Fresh horse tracks and dung spotted the dry ground. "Someone's been here." He stopped the wagon and they jumped to the ground examining the tracks. "Two riders in and out. Same tracks we found before." They climbed on the wagon and drove the team to the barn. "I'll get the animals settled, you check the area, chicken house first, that's what they raided last time."

Callum advanced toward the chicken coop, rifle in hand.

Daniel led the two horses to their stalls and gave them feed and water. "I'll be back and rub you down later." He glanced around the barn, knowing whoever invaded the property was long gone. The encounter with the Nelsons had him on edge, more for Sarah than himself. She might be able to fight off one of them, but they always traveled in twos. He'd be surprised if the young miss made it through the week. She'd be long gone by the time he went to town again, as she should. Wylder was no place for a fine lady.

Callum came in the barn. "Got two chickens this time, the brown one and the black and white speckled one. I didn't see anything else missing. Tool shed's still locked. Let's unload the wagon and I'll fix us some supper."

"I wouldn't mind some of your catheads." He stacked bags of oats against a wall. The men worked in silence until all the provisions for the horses, milk cow, pigs, and chickens were put in their place. He removed his hat and wiped sweat from his forehead. "I'm gonna give the horses a rubdown and brushing."

"Come to my cabin when you're done." Callum gathered the sack of flour and tub of lard. "Gotta milk the cow, I hear her bellowing."

Daniel went to work. He'd taken care of horses since he was old enough to hold a currycomb. They needed his care, but he craved the peace he experienced working with them. He came west to raise quarter horses even though Callum wanted to raise draft horses. Callum was a faithful friend and hell of a worker, but he didn't have any business sense. The money his father gave him to start his ranch was all they had, and he wouldn't gamble it on a whim. Red just missed Scotland and the black Friesian Stallion he had as a boy. He paid the man a good wage and supplied him with the best quarter horse they could find.

Kentucky snorted and tapped his hoof on the ground. "I'm coming, you spoiled brat." He placed two buckets in the stall, one with fresh water and the other with oats. The horse nudged him. He retrieved a knife from his pocket and cut pieces of an apple. "Don't tell the others." He spoke softly to his pet. "You're a fine fellow." Kentucky whinnied in response. "See you tomorrow, boy."

He rambled around the barn, house, and chicken coop. There were a few footprints, but he couldn't tell if they were from the robbers. People stealing food was a common occurrence, but horse stealing was a different matter. Horse theft and cattle rustling were both a hanging offense if the law caught you. Fellow rancher Caleb Holt told him stories of the ranchers who came before them who took matters into their hands and hung the perpetrators themselves.

He entered Callum's small house and the smell of fried pork fatback and coffee made his stomach growl. "Smells good, I'm starved."

Callum set a plate of butter and syrup in the middle of the kitchen table beside the platter of biscuits and bacon. "Take a seat."

Daniel helped himself to the food. "Guess someone was hungry and needed fried chicken for supper. Didn't see anything else disturbed."

"Nor I." Callum poured coffee into his cup.

"We need to be more vigilant. Don't want anyone stealing our horse stock." He buttered a biscuit and filled it with pork.

Callum advised him. "Better wear your gun belt for a while."

"After today, I'll wear it every time I leave the ranch." If Callum hadn't been with him today, he might be in Doc Sullivan's surgery right now. Or worse, dead. He contemplated the truth as they ate in silence.

He finished his meal and scooted his chair back from the table. "How's it going with the new stallion?"

"He'll be ready in a few weeks. Taking my time with him, but it'll be worth it." He removed their plates and put them in the sink.

Daniel pumped water and washed while Callum dried and stacked their dishware on the worktable. He left his friend and walked the short distance to his house. He couldn't shake the heaviness that settled on his chest since he left the young lady in Wylder. Widow Lowery wasn't a caring person and Sarah would have to fend for herself. She appeared well-off so maybe she had money to stay at one of the good hotels, but there was a vulnerability about her that bothered him, made him want to protect her. Could be he confused that with the fire in his belly that flamed when he gazed in her blue eyes. All the way home, he'd wanted to turn around and bring her to the ranch and take care of her, but he couldn't. Her aunt would have gossip spread over Wylder before he had the girl in his buggy.

He hastened through his house, checked the wall safe behind the landscape picture of a lake with a mountain in the distance. The art wasn't to his liking, but the dimensions covered the opening. He told no one, including Callum. Not that his friend would ever rob him, it was to keep him safe. Around here if certain people had any knowledge you had money; they'd hurt anyone close to you to have it. Assured nothing had been disturbed, he lit the kerosene lamp and sat at his desk. The figuring took his mind off the beautiful woman, for a little while. She was such a tiny thing and the sight of her trying to fend off the two men made him smile. He could still see her trying to knee old Jasper in the balls. He hated she'd missed her mark.

Chapter Three

Sarah stood at the window most of the night peeping into the street. The sounds of gunfire, men fighting, yelling, laughing, cussing, and the laughter of a woman being chased through the streets kept her awake. The only time in her life she'd been alone was in the sleeping car of the train. She had a room to herself at home, but her parents were just down the hall in theirs. The plan was to stay long enough for people in Savannah to move on to the next scandal, then return to the safety and peace of mind in her home.

She poured water from the pitcher into a bowl and washed her face. The room held no mirror, so she retrieved hers from the trunk and positioned it on the window ledge while she tackled her hair. The tangles from her fitful sleep caught in the comb but soon the long tresses were wound and attached to her head with the hair pin. She secured her hat with the ribbon tied under her chin.

A man turned a closed sign to open on the restaurant across the street. Her stomach growled a reminder she needed sustenance. The satin dress with the bustle rested on the chair. She stepped into it and fastened the front buttons, grabbed the drawstring bag, and filled it with coins, her key, lace handkerchief, and an essence bottle. Today she'd be ready for the rotten smells of cattle dung and nasty men.

She locked her door and checked the street before descending the stairs. The air was cool and the town quiet, a sharp contrast from the disorderly night. The sun had just started to rise, and she stared at the beauty of the sky. It was the bluest blue with orange streaks and not a white cloud to be seen. It was even more beautiful than the sunrise at her beloved Atlantic Ocean. She inhaled a deep breath, feeling renewed and brave, she held her head high and descended the steps. After a wagon and two men on horseback passed, she crossed the street. She put her hand on the doorknob and hesitated then walked inside as the tinkling of a bell signaled her arrival.

"Take a seat. Be right with ya." A man yelled from the back room.

She sat at a large table and examined the restaurant. Although the wooden tables and chairs were mismatched, the place was clean and tidy. Her eyes fell on a small table with two chairs. Her first time taking a meal by herself made her self-conscious. She stood and carefully placed the chair at the table and tiptoed to the smaller one. On the train, they'd been in close quarters and people sat together in the dining car. They shared a traveler's camaraderie of adventure. This was just plain lonesome.

The man appeared with a cup of coffee. "I'm Jake, I own this place. You new to town?"

She removed her gloves and placed them on the table. "I'm Sarah Miller from Savannah, Georgia, just visiting my Aunt Mildred."

Jake placed the cup of coffee on the table. "Mildred?"

"Widow Lowery. She and my mother are sisters."

She lifted the coffee cup and smelled the strong brew.

"Didn't know she had any family. I know she and her husband had no children. Sad about him dying but she seems to be able to take care of herself. Says a lot for a woman living alone and running a business in this town."

Sarah drank a sip of the black liquid. The steaming coffee burned her mouth, and the bitter taste made her gag. "I take my coffee with condensed milk."

"Condensed milk, huh? Bet that's a good combination but we ain't got none. I can bring you some sugar and fresh cow's milk." Four men entered the restaurant. Jake addressed them. "Ain't got no help today, one of my waitresses ran off with a trapper, don't expect her back. Have a seat." He addressed Sarah. "How you want your eggs?" He headed toward the kitchen.

She raised her voice, so he'd hear. "Scrambled, please."

She glanced at the four men who sat at the table she'd occupied. One of them winked. She pretended to rummage through her reticule when Jake returned with milk and sugar for her and cups of coffee for the men.

He returned to the kitchen and brought out a plate of food. "Here ya go miss. The plate overflowed with scrambled eggs, sausage, and a biscuit covered in gravy. She ate slowly at first until she could be sure no one noticed then she devoured the food as her stomach demanded.

The restaurant filled until every seat was taken, mostly by men. There were a few women dressed in plain work dresses. Jake hurried from table to table before retreating to the kitchen to prepare food. Men yelled for coffee refills and demanded breakfast.

Sarah walked into the kitchen. Jake had plates lined up on the counter filling each one with food. "No one allowed in the kitchen but me. I'll be right out."

The coffee pot rested on top of the wood stove. She grabbed a rag for the hot handle. "You have a crowd of hungry people demanding coffee. I need a job and you need help. I'm putting myself to work."

Jake considered her. "I don't employ fancy ladies, but I ain't got no choice today. You keep the coffee filled and take money. Breakfast is a dime. In your spare time take plates out." He continued pouring gravy on biscuits. "Take your hat off and if you last 'til tomorrow wear a different dress. The only women around here dress in that fashion work at the Social Club."

She held the hot pot of coffee and asked, "What's the Social Club?"

"It's the whore house on the other side of the tracks." He placed sausage on each plate. "Go." He wiped his hands on his apron.

She hesitated. The man who winked must have thought she'd worked all night at the brothel and now she had to serve him coffee. The assurance of going home soon spurred her into action. She entered the dining room and refilled coffee cups as Jake brought out plates. The men settled and ate their breakfast and occasionally yelled for coffee and more biscuits with syrup. When they were done, she sashayed around each table and collected ten cents from each person.

The restaurant held a few patrons after the breakfast rush. These men were dressed in suits and read newspapers while they ate. They were polite and reminded her of people from home. Through small talk she discovered they were lawyers, bankers, and a doctor. A few of the women owned or worked at businesses in town.

The lull between breakfast and lunch gave them just enough time to prepare for the next surge.

Jake stirred a pot of dried beans and removed the pans of cornbread from the oven as she entered the kitchen. "Here's the menu for lunch if anyone asks. Pot roast, pinto beans, spinach and cornbread. Indian pudding for dessert, coffee or tea. You keep the drinks flowing and help by taking plates out and collecting money, just like at breakfast. Lunch is twenty-five cents.

Her stomach rumbled at the smells escaping from the pots simmering on the stove.

Jake passed her a bowl of beans and a slice of cornbread. "Here, eat this, can't have you fainting from lack of food."

She leaned against the counter and savored the beans and bread. "Delicious, Jake. Who taught you how to cook?"

"Necessity, same way you learned how to be a waitress this morning." He smiled as he continued to work. "I can pay you a dollar a day. I need you Monday through Friday, my wife helps me on Saturday and Sunday, but she won't work every day."

Five dollars a week, she'd give two to her aunt and have three for necessities. "Thanks Jake, I'll take the job."

He stared. "Better fix your hair and sit for a minute before the crowd arrives, you look haggard."

She pulled the hair clip from her hair and smoothed

it back into a ball on the back of her head and pinned it in place. She sat and rubbed her toes, they ached from standing and walking. The velvet boots had no support for her feet; tomorrow she'd wear her leather shoes.

Soon the restaurant was full again, the experience she garnered from the morning boosted her confidence and she laughed and joked with the diners.

Sarah dried and put up the plates and utensils before making her way across the street. She entered Lowery's Dress Shoppe to tell her aunt about her new position.

"Where ya been all day?" Widow Lowery said as she stacked folded material on a shelf.

"Working, I got a job with Jake at the restaurant, waitressing." She found a bolt of white cotton fabric. "I need to make an apron for work. Can I buy enough of this and some thread?"

"Sure can." Mildred unrolled the material and cut enough for an apron. "Here's a needle and thread, no charge."

Sarah spotted a girl about her age standing in the corner. The girl was pretty but dressed in men's trousers and a shirt too big for her body.

Widow Lowery said. "Sarah, meet Leona Fabray, my wash woman. Can't support myself selling cloth so I take in washing. She lives in a room in the back."

She smiled at Leona and the girl glanced down. "Do you have a bathtub?" Sarah addressed her aunt. "I need to get the dirt and grime from the trip off my body."

The old lady nodded toward her employee. "We use the wash tub. Leona will help you. I'll cut the pattern pieces for your apron and have it ready for you."

She followed the girl to the back of the store. "Where's your room?"

Leona showed her to a tiny room with just enough space for her bed, dresser with a small mirror on a stand, and a chair. The dresser held a kerosene lamp and a bowl and pitcher. "Widow lets me stay here, she takes my board out of my pay. Says you're her niece. She ain't never talked about family a'fore."

The wash woman put water to boil over a fire and pulled the washtub inside.

Sarah sat in a chair, removed her shoes, and massaged her aching feet. "I've never been so tired in my life."

"If'n you want, I'll see what I can do 'bout gettin' the stain out of your dress," Leona said as she poured hot water in the tub.

She remembered the gravy stain she'd gotten when she almost dropped a plate of food. "Thank you."

The wash woman collected her dress after she stepped out of it and turned it over to examine the back. "I've seen the women wear bustle skirts." She stared at Sarah. "Though I never seen a chemise so fancy." The girl advanced closer and examined the fine lace and stitching. "Pity to hide the finery under your dress." She folded the clothes and placed them in the chair. "Better not dress this way if'n you want to fit in. Why'd you come to Wylder?"

She turned her back and stepped out of her clothing. "It's a long story, but I'm going back as soon as people from home move on to another person's misfortune."

The wash woman handed her some soap and a rag.

"Must have been something bad for you to come all the way out west."

She closed her eyes and relaxed in the small tub. "My mother and daddy thought so." The hot water soothed her aching bones, she soaked until the water got cold and her muscles cramped from the position. "This tub is small, how does Aunt Mildred fit into it?"

Leona passed her a thick drying cloth and extended her hand to assist her out. "Oh, she doesn't fit in this here tub. She fills it with water and stands next to it washin' herself."

Sarah put her clothes on as the girl pushed the tub to the exit and poured the water outside. "I don't know anyone in Wylder except my aunt. I hope we can be friends."

"Yes'm, sure can." Leona said as she cleaned up the floor with Sarah's drying cloth. "Sure can."

Sarah walked the stairs, turned the key, and placed the chair under the knob. She sewed the apron together and smoothed the wrinkles out of her plain dress and draped it across the trunk. Her shoes and stockings readied along with her apron for the coming day at the restaurant. Gun shots still rang out during the night, but she was too exhausted to care.

Chapter Four

Daniel immersed himself in paperwork he'd avoided for months and backbreaking physical ranch work in order to forget the young woman from Savannah. It worked during the day, but at night dreams of her interrupted his sleep. It had been a long time since a woman as refined as she had graced Wylder. The need to check on her spurred him to action. He saddled Kentucky and rode by the corral where Callum shoed horses. "Going to town this morning, need anything?"

Callum placed the hoof nippers on the ground and walked toward his friend. "Ye be wearin' a new shirt and ye washed yer hair."

"I washed my hair because it was dirty, and I haven't done my washing this week. This is my last clean shirt." He steadied Kentucky who pranced in a circle.

Callum grabbed the farrier rasp and ambled back to his charge. "No, don't need a thing from town but I dinnae ken why you haven't been back to see the lass before now." A grin played over his face.

He turned Kentucky toward town. "I don't know what you're talking about, Red."

As he rode away, Callum's strong baritone voice sang a Scottish folk song. Something about giving his love ribbons and taking her down to her chamber.

He let the horse gallop and release its pent-up energy. Breeding racehorses with his father back home taught him horses need the freedom to feel the breeze through their mane. He slowed Kentucky to a canter and settled into the saddle. He pondered if he was doing the right thing. Sarah wasn't the type of woman to remain in Wylder, Wyoming. Hell, he figured she'd not made it through the week. Probably already left on the next stage after her encounter with the Nelsons. And her staying with Widow Lowery. The old woman, her aunt, how could that be? The sassy woman held her own in town and ran a much-needed business, but she wasn't the welcoming sort. If Sarah stayed, the old lady wouldn't make it easy for her.

Daniel rode into town and tied the reins to a hitching post in front of the bank. Across the street men gathered around two women. He pushed his way through the crowd and spotted Sarah and Leona Fabray surrounded by miners and railroad workers. "Oh, shit, not again." This time he wore his gun belt. He pulled his revolver and strutted toward the girls.

Sarah yelled and stomped her foot. "Let us be."

The men laughed and moved closer. A brave one tugged at her dress. "Never felt such material before. Mighty pretty. Where you from, little lady?"

He fired a shot into the air. The men trampled each other as they scattered. He searched faces for the Nelsons and was relieved he didn't see them.

He holstered his gun. "They didn't hurt you two, did they?"

Leona answered. "Oh, Mr. Taylor, they would'na hurt me but it was Sarah they were after."

He stared at the woman dressed in yet another fine

silk dress. The turquoise color made her blue eyes appear green; the bustle accented her tiny waist with a bodice cut low to show the creamy skin of her ample bosom. "Allow me to say something, Miss Miller?"

Sarah tugged her gloves. "By all means."

He removed his hat and held it in his hand. "You'll have a problem in this town if you keep going out unescorted dressed in this fashion. I'm sure all ladies in Savannah dressed in finery and lace." A tear fell from her eye and he studied her face to decide if he'd enraged her or saddened her. "I'm sorry, I didn't mean to offend you."

She stood straighter and glared. "I own one plain dress and it's dirty from working all week. I'll get another made when I get enough money saved for cloth."

"You have a job? Where?" She had more gumption than he gave her credit for. He'd give her money for a dress, but she appeared to be too proud, so he'd let the offer pass, for now.

"I'm a waitress at Jake's Place. I've worked every day since I arrived in town. If you'll excuse us, we need to go in the apothecary and get the liniment for Widow Lowery's rheumatism."

He stepped aside and let them pass, then waited on a bench in front of the bakery. She was feisty and strong; he liked a woman with spunk. The apothecary door opened, and he stood. "I'll escort you to the dress shop."

She nodded toward Leona. "We'll be fine. No need."

He removed his hat and straightened the brim. "Wanted to ask." He raised his head and continued.

"Are you hungry?" Her damn eyes were pools of turquoise water pulling him under. He put his hat on his head and captured her hand. "I'm buying you a meal."

Leona reached for the sack. "I'll git this back to the widow 'fore she has my hide."

"Thank you," she called after the girl who ran across the street, then addressed the gentleman. "Can we eat anywhere but Jake's? I've eaten there every day this week."

"We'll eat at the Vincent House Hotel, they have excellent food and it's fancier, more to your taste, I'm sure." He waited for a wagon to pass before guiding her across the street. "You're dressed in the appropriate attire for the hotel dining room."

She held on to his arm. "I didn't think you liked my dress."

"Didn't say I didn't like it, said if you went out alone dressed in that fashion, you'd have a problem." He winked at her. "You aren't alone, now. You're with me." He returned her smirk with a smile.

They were seated at a table for two by the window. The waitress gave them a menu and he sat his aside while she studied hers. "I think you'll find this to your liking. The beef tenderloin is superb."

She put her menu next to his. "Sounds delicious. This reminds me of a place in Savannah."

"When do you plan to return?" He waited for her answer, but she said nothing. "Figured you'd already left on this week's stage."

She lowered her voice so only he could hear. "I need to stay in this godforsaken place a while longer."

"You running from something or someone?" He leaned toward her. "What caused you to leave your home?"

The waitress appeared at their table. "What can I bring you?" She picked up their menus.

"Bring us chicken soup, first, then the beef tenderloin and some of your good rolls." He glanced at his date. "Good for you?"

"Yes," she smiled at the older lady who took their order.

He waited until the woman was out of earshot. "You were saying?"

She leaned forward. "I was engaged to be married. My fiancé appeared to be a gentleman, he promised me a good life, said he had enough money to take care of me—even showed me a house he bought for us. The day of our wedding, he didn't show. I stood at the back of the church waiting for over an hour. I later found out he was a deceiver who'd drifted into Savannah from somewhere in Florida. The night before our wedding he got drunk at the tavern boasted to all who would listen how he'd bedded a virgin. No one's seen him since, but his disappearance didn't stop people from spreading gossip. I figure I'll go home when they move on to the next scandal."

If this woman let him take her to bed, he'd not leave her, ever. "I'm sorry, there are some villainous men in this world, just as there are evil women."

"Why is it I seem to draw the wrong men?" She put her hand to her mouth. "I'm sorry, I didn't mean to declare you're a bad person. You've been nothing but the gentleman. Seems every time you're in town, you're rescuing me."

He cursed himself for his impure thoughts about her. "I understand. He did you wrong and now you've been exposed to abuse by worse men." The carnal ideas of her in his bed took a while to dissipate. Her past made him want to protect her, her beauty made him want to love her, her intellect made him want to share his dreams with her every damn day. But her body made him want to explore and please her. He examined Sarah with his eyes. She was a woman made for fancy clothes and she wore them well. No wonder she had every man in town bewitched.

"Where are you from? You don't talk or act like others in this town." She tugged her gloves carefully from each finger to prevent stretching the fabric.

"Back east, Lexington, Kentucky to be exact. Lived in Wylder for five years. I own a ranch just outside town where I raise quarter horses. Guess you want to know why, too." He gave her a smile while wanting to taste her pink lips and touch her skin to see if it was as soft as it appeared.

"Yes, I do want to know why a handsome man who seems to be educated and know better ended up in Wylder." She waited for his response.

He put the sentences together in his head before he spoke. It was a long story, and he didn't want to monopolize the conversation and make it about him. "I came with a friend who worked for my family. They breed and sell racehorses. After college I craved adventure. My father had a desire to travel to the west but realized he was too old. My mother didn't want to leave her home and they both agreed they couldn't sell the business he inherited from his father. He gave me money to buy a ranch, Callum was ready for another adventure, so we ended up in Wyoming." He watched her wrap the chain of her necklace around her finger.

The stone was real and the chain gold. Scandal or not, she was a woman of means and didn't belong in Wylder, Wyoming.

She gazed in his eyes and hesitated before she asked. "What did you study in college?"

"Law." Her nervous tangling of the jewelry drew his attention to the mounds rising from her bodice. She seemed genuinely interested in his life. He considered a room upstairs where they could get to know each other even better. It had been too damn long since he held a woman of her caliber. Not since Becca. "Did you get extra schooling?"

"Mrs. Patterson's Finishing School." She stood and curtsied.

He loved her impromptu action. He loved everything about this girl. She had no idea how funny and adorable she was.

After they finished their soup, the waitress brought plates laden with beef and vegetables. He couldn't believe a small woman could eat as much as Sarah. She devoured the rolls along with all the food on her plate. "How about dessert?" he asked.

"Oh, yes. I do have a sweet tooth." She dabbed her mouth with the napkin.

Daniel signaled for the waitress. "Do you have chess pie today?"

The woman stacked the plates and removed them from their table. "Yes sir, we do."

"We'll each have a piece of pie. Thank you." He waited until the waitress left the table then addressed his date. "I know you don't plan to stay, but I want to see you while you're in Wylder. Won't be a problem with your aunt, will it?"

She shook her head. "Widow Lowery doesn't care what I do as long as I pay her room and board every week. Her life is so different from Mama's, but I don't think she'd want it any other way. After her husband died, Mother sent her a letter and begged her to move to Savannah, but she refused, said she had a home in Wyoming."

"I think she makes more money off her washing service than she does dressmaking, she has a much-needed business in this town." He pulled out paper money and counted through the bills. "So you'll agree to my courting you?"

She placed her napkin on the table and put on her gloves. "I'd like that very much, and thank you for the delicious lunch. I never imagined a town in the west would have a restaurant with food to rival Savannah."

He stood and pulled out her chair. "Glad you enjoyed it. We'll do this again." He put his hat on and escorted her. "I'll walk you back. Any more trouble with the Nelsons?"

She walked outside, he trailed close behind. "I've seen them hanging around, but they haven't approached me. I make sure to secure the lock and check the street before I leave my room."

"Best to be cautious." He guided her across the street to the dress shop. He paused and stared at her mouth. The urge to kiss her lips tempted him, instead he raised her gloved hand to his lips and brushed a kiss over it. "Until next time."

"Yes." She stepped into the store.

Daniel walked to the bank to do business with Mr. Mountroy. He didn't keep all his money in the bank, didn't trust them, just kept enough to use as collateral if he needed a loan. His father taught him to use other people's money but pay it back on time and don't borrow what you can't pay back. The plan had worked, thus far he'd made and saved more money than he dreamed possible raising quarter horses. With the abundance of cash, he was able to pay Callum a good salary and even contemplated making him a partner in the business.

Chapter Five

Sarah entered the dress shop and leaned against the wall. A deep sigh escaped her lips, the memory of the kiss that grazed her hand brought a smile. A grunt from her aunt pulled her back to the present. Widow Lowery observed the goings on from the window of her store and spread gossip like fire in a dry forest. "See you ain't wasted no time finding a gentleman caller." The old woman stepped from behind the cutting table.

She hadn't forgotten men were forbidden, but she had to have a little fun. "He approached me at the apothecary and offered to buy me a meal."

Mildred stacked fabric on a shelf. "Never heard nothin' bad about Daniel Taylor, seems to be a good man. I know he rescued you the day you arrived. Ain't no secrets in this town. Ain't many young, available, attractive women either. I'd hate to see Mr. Taylor court you and think he's got a future and then you up and leave."

Sarah stared at the floor, too embarrassed to meet the widow's eyes. Her mother called her frivolous and maybe she was, but she found Daniel's company pleasant. He didn't expect her to stay so why should she have any concerns he would want anything more than friendship? "I've been honest with him. I told him everything, he knows I want to go back home, and I will."

Her aunt placed thread rolls on the wall pegs. "Leona's out back if that's who you came in here for."

She hurried through the store and stepped outside. The wash woman stirred a large pot of men's underwear. The stench of the dirty clothes and the water heating over a fire made her feel sorry for her new friend. Leona worked long, hard hours and the room she stayed in was no larger than their water closet at home.

The washer woman sat a chair beside the large pot. "Sit a spell and tell me 'bout your time with Mr. Taylor."

Sarah sat, removed her hat, and took the pin out of her hair. "I like him. He's…" She searched for the right word. "He's real kind."

"I like to look at 'im." Leona stood and hung a pair of long johns on the line. "Never seen a man so purdy."

"He's handsome." Sarah corrected. "Women are pretty, men are handsome."

"You gonna court 'im?" She filled a small pot with hot water and added it to the wash pot.

Sarah ran her hands through her hair and wound it around her head. "Yes, I think I'll court him. I'm going to see Miss Adelaide Willowby and offer my services to the women at the Wylder County Social Club." She pinned her hair and secured the hat.

Leona dropped a man's shirt on the ground. "What you talkin' 'bout? Don't let Widow Lowery find out you're goin' to the whorehouse." She picked up the shirt and shook the dirt off.

Sarah smoothed her dress and put on her gloves. "It was her idea, she told me the day I arrived the only way I could make money with embroidery would be for the women at the Social Club."

"I don't think she meant for ya to call on 'em." She stepped in front of her. "Don't go, Miss Sarah."

"I could wait until you're finished, and you could accompany me," she offered, hoping the girl would say yes. The apprehension of meeting the madam alone was almost as strong as the fear of the woman rejecting her business deal.

"Widow will have my hide if she found out I went there. She'll have yours, too."

"I'm not afraid of my aunt, besides, no sense in me lazing around on my off days when I could make money doing something." She made her way around the back of the building and hastened toward Buckboard Alley not wanting to be seen by Mildred.

The sight of the Social Club had greeted her from the window of the train when she arrived in Wylder. She believed it would be a fun place to spend time and meet people. In Savannah, she and her friends met every week to discuss books, the latest fashions, and music. From Jake she learned the social club was the whorehouse Widow Lowery talked about.

She approached the establishment. A striking dark-haired woman sat in a rocker on the porch. Sarah walked proud with her head high and strutted straight to the door. She knocked. No one answered. She wanted to tuck her tail and run. This was a stupid idea. She had no business here but the desperation for money won out.

The lady spoke. "You need something?"

She rapped the door knocker. "Need to see Miss Willowby." Sarah steadied her hand on the doorknob.

"Don't," the woman commanded. "Knock again,

someone will let you in."

She drew her hand back. Of course, she couldn't barge in. She knocked again and the door opened.

An older woman stood before her. "May I help you?"

"Miss Adelaide Willowby?" Sarah stared at the woman, she was older than she expected the madam would be and her accent reminded her of Callum.

"Heavens, no, dear. I'm Miss McCarthy." She stepped aside. "Come in, lovely."

She entered and gazed around the house. A large Negro man stood to the right with his arms crossed over his chest. Sarah almost jumped out of her skin. He glared. She peered from him to the older lady. "My name is Sarah Miller and I'm here to see Miss Willowby."

"Is she expecting you?" the woman asked.

"No, but I need to talk with her if she's available." A beautiful petite woman with the largest breasts and the tiniest waist she'd ever seen came into the room. Several diamond necklaces adorned her neck. The light blue dress accented the woman's blond hair. She couldn't find her voice.

Miss McCarthy stepped aside. "This is Sarah Miller; says she needs to talk to you."

"Come on back to my office. You're a pretty little thing. Just get into town?" The madam entered her sitting room.

Sarah followed; the material of her dress clinched in her hands. "Yes, I haven't been in town long." She struggled to keep her knees from shaking. "I want to talk to you about a job."

The lady studied the young woman and turned her

around so she could see her from all angles. "I'll need references." The woman sat at her desk and motioned for her to sit in a chair.

She sat straight as an arrow and placed her hands in her lap. "I can get some references from the people I worked for back home."

"Where's home and why do you want a job with us?" Miss Adelaide leaned back in her chair.

"I'm from Savannah, I arrived in Wylder last week. My Aunt, I mean Widow Lowery suggested I call on you and offer my services." Sarah glanced around the beautifully decorated room.

"Your aunt is Widow Lowery?" Miss Adelaide put her hands under her chin and smiled.

"Yes, she's my mother's sister." The smell of rose perfume permeated the air and filled her nostrils. It reminded her of her mother's dressing room, and she was suddenly homesick.

"Lowery's Dress Shoppe makes most of our dresses. Mildred doesn't condone what we do, but she always takes our money. I'm surprised she sent you to us." The proprietress stood and gazed out the window.

"I am quite good at what I do, I learned the skills from my mother. She was the best in Savannah, everyone in town enjoyed her talents. She said I had an aptitude for it from a young age, I've won contests for my proficiency and expertise. Widow Lowery says she has no use for it in the store and I should see you." Sarah addressed the lady with hope in her voice.

Miss Adelaide turned and raked her eyes over Sarah. "Well, you are quite sure of yourself. I admire someone with confidence. Men do, too. I do have an opening for another girl, you'll have your own room which you'll use for your work. I have strict rules here and everyone follows them. At first, you'll be the girl all the men want because you're new and very pretty."

Sarah jumped from the chair; her hands clenched into fists at her side. "Men? I'm not a whore."

The madam sat in her chair brandishing a composed smile. "You have it all wrong, dear. I don't run a whore house, I run a social club. Men come here for companionship. What is it you are here for, my dear, if not a job as a consort to the men in town?"

"Embroidery." She grabbed the sides of the chair and sat. Her eyes met the lady's and they both burst out laughing. Their giggles turned into raucous laughter which made her belly ache. The guffaw died down and they smiled at each other. At that moment she wished she were one of Miss Adelaide's girls. "Guess I better explain myself." Sarah's confidence drove her. "Widow Lowery says you're the only one in town who would be interested in paying for embellishments on your dresses. I am quite good at the skill of embroidery and I know how to make lace, so if you require my services, you can find me at Jake's Place where I waitress, or in my room above the dress shop."

In a hurry to leave, she stood.

Miss Addie remained seated; her hands clasped together resting on the desk. "Sarah, there is just one reason you would leave your home and come to Wylder, Wyoming. Are you running from a man or to one?"

At the madam's question, she inhaled a deep breath. "You are a very observant woman."

"In my line of work, it's a requirement." Miss Adelaide stood.

Her eyes met Miss Willowby's. "There was a scandal, I'm in town until it settles."

"Best of luck to you, I'm sure I'll be calling on you for your services." She stretched her hand out.

Sarah shook the woman's hand. "Thank you."

The madam crossed the room and opened the door. "I'll be in touch."

Sarah nodded and came face to face with the large man.

He stepped back and let her go ahead. "My name is Abraham. I'll see you out."

Heat emanated from his body. He was tall, handsome and the largest man she'd ever seen. She wished he could walk her back and protect her as he did the girls at the Social Club.

She exited the house and crossed the railroad tracks. She chuckled to herself at the misunderstanding but wondered how such beautiful women would sell their body to please a man. Her experience with James confirmed what she'd overheard her mother and women of town say. Men needed sex and their job as wives was to endure it. She'd suffered through the act with James, the first time hurt so much she cried. The second time, she'd almost arrived. She was climbing, soaring, ascending beyond someplace, somewhere, almost there and James groaned and rolled off her. She asked him about her body's response, and he laughed. Now she was suffering for her stupidity and Miss Willowby speculated she'd want to do that for a living. Not likely.

She passed the Calvary Office and a young officer sat on a bench. He smiled and said "Hello." She presented him with a wide smile and moved on, anxious to tell Leona of her news. She could support herself and make it in this town alone, the awareness bubbled inside her.

Jasper Nelson stepped in front of her. "What you doin' goin' to the whore house? I know'd you weren't no innocent." He grabbed her arm and pulled her close.

"Let go of me." Her effort to push his chest with her hands were futile. Today she didn't miss her mark. She brought her knee up and found the target.

The man doubled over. "I'll get you for this, bitch."

She held back a scream, raised her skirt and ran as fast as her legs would allow until she reached the back of the dress shop.

Leona stood at the pot stirring clothes. "Why you runnin'?"

Sarah staggered to the chair, expecting Jasper to appear any minute. She sucked air into her lungs to calm her trembling body and settled in the seat.

The wash girl got on her knees in front of her. "What happened?" She grabbed a rag and wet it then rubbed Sarah's face. "Was it bad at the Social Club? What'd they do to ya?"

She found her voice. "Miss Adelaide is a genuinely nice woman. She's going to give me work." She wiped her eyes. "Jasper Nelson. He grabbed me. He means me harm, I know it."

"How'd you get away?" Leona asked.

"I did what my father told me to do if I was alone and needed protection. I took my knee to his testicle." She passed the rag to Leona.

The girl stared. "What's a testicle?"

"A part of a man's anatomy between his legs. It's very tender. Papa said hurting a man there is how a woman can get away from someone who tries to hurt her." Sarah stood. Her legs quivered under her weight. She paraded around the small yard to gain her bearings.

"I thought they was balls. Done that a couple times myself when a drunk got frisky with me." Leona added soap to the pot. "Tell me about the Social Club. Did you see anything or anybody, you know, doing something?"

"No, it's pretty inside the house. Decorated with beautiful paintings and tapestries." She stepped away from the heat to fill her lungs with fresh air. "Miss Adelaide says it's just a social club where men come and spend time with the ladies."

She put her hands on her hips. "Ain't what I heard."

Sarah's legs finally felt steady and she walked toward the shop. "Believe what you want, just telling you what I observed today."

"Wait, here's yer dress." Leona called after her. "I got the stain out."

Sarah took the dress, turning it in her hands as she searched for the smudge. "Well, I'll be, you did. Good work."

She trudged up the stairs scanning the street for Jasper. She probably hadn't seen the last of the Nelsons and the realization scared her more than she'd admit.

Chapter Six

Daniel finished his business at Goldmount Bank, untied Kentucky's reins and mounted the horse. He rode down Sidewinder Lane hoping for a glimpse of Sarah. The girl from Savannah made him hope again and he didn't know if he should travel that road.

Sarah would leave just like the others and he'd be alone. His mother wanted to send him a mail order bride. Promised to interview them and send the prettiest and smartest of the lot. In his mind, Sarah was the prettiest and smartest, although very naive.

He could see how a fast-talking man could take advantage of her. He wanted to find the bastard and shoot him but then if the incident had never happened, the fancy girl wouldn't be in Wylder. His mother even wrote Callum and offered the same services. The Scotsman laughed, saying "I don't need a woman, I've got all I can handle at The Wylder Social Club. I get what I want and don't have to hear any griping or complaining from a woman all week."

Daniel had only visited the brothel one time. He'd been entertained by an older woman whose tricks he still remembered. By far the best sex he'd ever experienced but the lack of intimacy and affection left him wanting. His skin craved the touch of Sarah's body. He slowed the horse as he passed a meadow just starting to grass and imagined lying with her there. He would be tender until their bodies could take no more and he'd... What the hell was he doing? He was no better than the man who jilted her. He spurred Kentucky to a fast trot and didn't slow until he turned into the lane toward the ranch. The speed and wind helped to calm the turmoil rolling in his brain. He stopped in front of his house. Callum sat on the front porch with a cup in his hand.

He dismounted and tied the reins to the hitching post. "Started drinking early, I see."

Callum downed the liquid. "Just water, I'll wait 'til after the Social Club to have a drink at the saloon. Don't want nothing to impede me performance, dinnae ken."

Daniel leaned against the porch rail. "I had lunch with Sarah Miller."

"Figured ye did. Find out why she drifted to Wylder?"

"Said she was abandoned at the altar by her fiancé. She needs to stay until her town moves on to another person's public embarrassment."

"Why don't ye come with me. The Social Club is the best place to let off some steam." He placed the cup on the rail.

"I just got home from Wylder, not going back. Enjoy yourself and keep your wits about you at the saloon." Daniel untied the reins and escorted Kentucky toward the barn.

Callum stood. "I'll keep me wits tonight. Plan to win some money at poker." He followed Daniel. "Besides, I can hold my liquor better than the rest."

"I don't want to have to get you out of jail, Red." Daniel guided his horse to the stable, unbuckled the cinch, and removed the saddle and bridle.

Callum mounted Finlay. "One time and it wasn't me fault. Sheriff said so."

Daniel turned his attention to Kentucky. He curried the horse and removed the dust and dirt from his legs. His loneliness and want of a woman had him thinking on things he had no right to think. His heart demanded one thing, his head another and his lower body part yelled for attention, he'd so long ignored. He poured oats into a trough and filled a bucket with water. He ran his hand over the smooth coat. "Good boy, Kentucky. Rest up, we're going back to town tomorrow."

****

Daniel rode toward Wylder with biscuits, deer jerky and a johnnycake along with a metal flask of Kentucky mash and a canteen of water. If it was in the cards, he planned to take Sarah on a picnic, spend time with her and get to know her better. With the buggy parked in front of the dress shop and Kentucky's reins tied to the post, he ran up the steps two at a time before he lost his nerve. He gazed around town to check if anyone noticed him before he rapped on the door. The sound of a chair moving across the floor and a click in the lock had him anxious to see the girl.

She opened the door enough to talk but not enough to let him in. "Daniel, this is a surprise."

He pushed his way inside, pulled her into his arms and kissed her. He'd craved this all week. Her small body fit his the way he knew it would, her kiss tasted sweet as he knew it would and her hair smelled of lilacs, the lasting scent that had stayed with him since their first encounter. He didn't expect the rejection as she pushed away and squirmed. He hesitated and

47

attempted to step back but at that moment she surrendered and returned the kiss. She'd not tied up her hair and it flowed down her back. He ran his hands through the silky strands and tugged her head while his tongue entered her sweet mouth.

She pressed her body closer, her bosom heaving against his chest. He opened his eyes; the small bed had his attention. He could make love to her right now, make her his, take her to the preacher, marry her. Then what? Sarah Miller, socialite from Savannah, Georgia would be happy living a solitary life on a ranch, with him?

He pulled back but held her in his arms and toyed with her hair. It was so damn soft; she was so damn soft. She smelled as fresh and sweet as a spring lilac. "I came to take you on a picnic."

She stepped back and ran her hands over the button on his shirt. "I accept your offer. Let me put my hair up and get my hat."

He kissed the top of her head. "Do you mind leaving your hair down? I prefer it."

She tugged her hat on and grabbed her gloves and reticule.

"Better bring a shawl, it's cool this morning." He glanced down the street to make sure no one drifted about. "After you."

She put the key in his hand, and he secured the lock before escorting her down the steps. "Want to show you some of the beautiful scenery of Wyoming. I've never been to Savannah but have been to Charleston, they say the towns are similar. You won't see any ocean here but the sunrises and sunsets and the snow in the winter when it covers the mountains, well,

Savannah doesn't have that."

She placed her hand in his. He situated her in the buggy. After a glance in the window of the dress shop, he tipped his hat to Widow Lowery and made his way to the other side of the carriage. "Your aunt doesn't appear happy this morning."

She tugged her gloves. "She's not keen on me seeing you. She likes you, says you're a good man and I shouldn't spend time with you since I plan to go back to Savannah."

Daniel guided the buggy out of town. "None of her business." Kentucky pranced; the horse was a show-off. He didn't use the small buggy often and the quarter horse enjoyed being in front pulling the carriage. He headed toward his farm, but they wouldn't stop there. He wasn't ready to show her the ranch yet. He drove toward a stand of pines and tied the reins to a tree before helping Sarah out of the buggy. "We'll walk to the creek and sit a spell." He lifted her to the ground. She weighed less than some of the feed bags he tossed in the barn. His lips found hers and he kissed her until Kentucky neighed. He released her. "Damn horse thinks he should get all the attention."

She approached the animal and ran her hand over his neck. "Kentucky, you are handsome, too."

He grinned. *She thinks I'm handsome*. He grabbed a wooden box while Sarah babied the horse. "Spoiled as hell, but he's good, one of the best I've owned. Raised him from a colt and trained him myself. I've got this country's best quarter horses on the ranch. We'll go riding, sometime."

She turned and faced him. "Oh, I don't ride."

He led her toward the creek. "Everyone needs to

know how to ride a horse."

Twigs cracked under their feet as they made their way to the bank. He unfolded a quilt and placed it on the ground. "I didn't have much food in the house, but I brought what I had. Made some biscuits and johnnycakes this morning so they're fresh."

"You cook?" She took a bite of jerky.

He bit a piece of the dried meat and chewed. "Callum and I make do. He's got a cabin on the ranch and I have my house. We share the chores; he cooks better than I do, so I eat with him most of the time." He handed her the canteen, and she drank the water. "Brought some whiskey." He showed her the flask.

She tipped back the metal container and took a sip.

He grabbed the flacon. "Careful, this is for sipping. Brought it to warm us if the breeze gets too cool."

"Heavens." She put her hand on her throat. "That burns, but it tastes good." She took the flask from him and sipped the bourbon. "I like it." She hiccupped.

He drank from the flacon and placed it in his pocket. "I believe you've had enough." She scooted close and he put his arm around her. A drop of water dripped on his sleeve. He searched the sky for more drops. She sobbed and more tears fell, he put both arms around her and stroked her hair. "Do you miss your parents?"

"Yes, but that's not why I'm upset." She sniffled and rubbed her face with the back of her hand.

He pulled a cloth from his pocket. He cleaned the water from her face. "Are you afraid of me? I won't hurt you."

She clung to his chest. "I only feel safe when I'm with you."

"I know it's hard for you living in Wylder." He smoothed her hair. It was hard for him to leave her in town alone with no protection.

"I ran into Jasper Nelson yesterday. He grabbed me and attempted to do inappropriate things to me." She blotted another tear.

Daniel's jaw tightened and he imagined all the things he would do to the bastard. His hands fisted as scenarios of beating the shit out of Jasper and his brother Silus played in his mind. If he laid one hand on his girl, he'd kill the bastard graveyard dead. "Did he do anything to you?" He demanded.

"No, I fought back. This time my dress was accommodating, and I hit my mark. He stumbled back cursing and I ran."

He pushed her hair from her shoulder and turned her face so he could gaze into her eyes. "Took a lot of nerve to face Jasper. I'm proud of you." He didn't want to tell her the man wouldn't back down. A woman bested him, and the humiliation didn't sit well with his kind. He stood and pulled her to her feet. "Let's stretch our legs." They sashayed arm in arm to the creek bank. The water babbled over the rocks; a pine needle flowed with the current. He wondered where it would end up.

"It's so peaceful." She paced along the edge. "In good weather, I'd spend my afternoons sitting by the river watching the ships. My friends and I sat and gossiped with our parasols and hats to keep the sun from burning us." She turned to face him. "In a million years, I could never imagine a town like Wylder. It's so far removed from Savannah. But next to the stream with you, I feel the same peace."

The water trickled over the rocks and the fish

jumped from the stream. She put her arm around his neck and brought his head down to hers. He kissed her thoroughly, his arms circled her body and drew her close. Their tongues tangled in their own dance. He'd dreamed about her skin and wanted to find out if it was as soft as her hair. He put his hand on her neck and let it drift to the mound of breast trapped by her dress. Her soft silky skin enticed him to explore every inch of her. He wanted, God he wanted, he wanted to strip her from her dress and taste her nipple and suck until she begged him to take her. He kissed her neck and made his way to the skin on her chest.

She tugged the leather cord from the back of his hair and threaded her hands through his mane. "I prefer your hair down, too."

He led her to the quilt and laid her on the ground, kissing her. She sat and tugged him toward her.

His hand slid to her breast. His mouth found her soft skin trying to escape her dress while he teased her nipple with his thumb. She groaned and pulled him beside her.

Her body would restore him, fix the broken fragments Becca left behind and he wanted to fit the pieces together right damn now. His erection ached to make her his. She touched his cheek with such tenderness and her quiet whimper drove him and stopped him at the same time. This gentle, precious woman captured his heart the first time he laid eyes on her. He adjusted himself in his pants and pulled her up to sit beside him. Not today, he told himself. "Sorry, I got carried away, been a long time since I was with a woman and never one that equaled you."

She placed her hand on his cheek and turned his

head toward her. "I had no idea kissing could be so…" She cast her eyes away from him. "So beautiful."

A tear slid from her eye and he wiped it away. "Did I hurt you?"

She reached for his hand. "No, you could never hurt me. Never had anyone love me the way you just did."

He pulled her close and kissed the top of her head. "Guess we better head back to town."

She helped him fold the quilt and put the remainder of the food in the box. "I had a wonderful time. I hope we can do it again."

He put his arm around her waist and guided her up the hill. "We will. I want to continue to call on you if you don't mind."

"I don't mind at all." She walked close beside him until they arrived at the buggy.

He climbed in the seat beside her and gave her a lingering kiss. He memorized the feel of her lips and the taste of her mouth. The bourbon lingered on her tongue. Two of his favorites—her, and Kentucky whiskey. He ended the embrace and without a word gathered the leads and guided the carriage toward town.

Chapter Seven

The late afternoon sun dropped toward the horizon as the carriage rolled into town. Sarah sighed and resigned herself to another lonely night as the horse made its way down Old Cheyenne Road into Wylder. The smell of horse dung and hay greeted her from the livery along with the sound of Dugan hammering hot metal on his anvil. The carriage slowed for the right turn on Sidewinder Lane signaling the end of their time together.

Daniel stopped the buggy and helped her out. "Thank you for a wonderful day." She gazed in his eyes. His hair, free of its cord, framed his handsome face. A kiss would top off the day but too many people passed along the street.

He brought her hand to his lips. "Thank you for allowing me to spend the day with you." He pressed a kiss to her palm. "Want me to escort you upstairs?"

"No, I'll be fine." She walked toward her room, each stairstep brought her to the confinement and isolation of her small quarters. Today with Daniel, she'd forgotten about her desperate existence. Her eyes focused on the large basket on the stoop. An envelope with her name on it sat on top of plain white fabric. She unlocked her door and turned to wave goodbye. He tipped his hat. The buggy drifted out of sight leaving the ache in her chest as empty as the street.

She gazed at the town and checked the corner of the buildings for anyone who would pose a danger then placed the basket on her bed. With the door closed, locked, and secured with the chair and a quick glance out the window for anyone lurking in the shadows, she removed her hat and gloves. Fear of the men and the gunshots in the night made for a fitful sleep. The dirty miners unnerved her, but they seemed harmless compared to Jasper and Silus. She'd be home soon, back in her bed down the hall from her parents. Safe. She would never take security for granted again.

Assured no bad men observed her enter the room alone, she opened the envelope and read the note.

Sarah,
This is a shawl I ordered from New York. It's one of my favorites but has always been too plain for my taste. I want you to create a floral design. I trust you to choose the best colors.
Miss Adelaide

Underneath the wrappings was a beautiful black wool shawl with black lace edging. She placed it around her body and inhaled the scent of roses. With the button secured, the cape cascaded around her body and enabled her to study the craftsmanship. The collar was made from the same lace as the bottom edging. The shawl must have cost a fortune.

The madam tested her, and she wanted to prove she could do the work. Sarah spread the cape on the bed and envisioned roses along the entire bottom. The design would be pretty, but it would take away from the fancy lace. A search through her trunk revealed her sewing kit with embroidery hoop, needles, floss, and small scissors. She turned the scissors over in her hand and decided to keep these next to her bed, they would make a good weapon if needed. Next was a quick check through the patterns for something appropriate.

The best floral style for this shawl would be roses. The beautiful madam epitomized the elegant flower. The best choice as far as she was concerned was the medium size flower combined with a green vine. A simple design placed on the front from the collar down to the hem on both sides of the opening of the cape would be beautiful. She placed different colors of thread on the black material to judge each color.

Sarah opened her curtains for better light and sat in the chair to study the hues. The afternoon sun made her sleepy and her eyes drifted closed. The hours spent with Daniel and what they did flashed through her mind. His actions were forceful but tender. When he pushed his way into her room and kissed her, he took possession of her and she let him. At that moment and by the creek, she would have given herself, she wanted to. James dominated her and coerced her by deception. With Daniel, she submitted but he was the strong one, she recognized the fire in his eyes. His manhood begged for her, but he let her go. Did he know how close she was to surrender?

Sarah rested between sleep and awake and relived each moment of her day until a knock and Leona's voice got her attention. She searched for the key and found it on the floor, placed the chair beside the bed and invited the girl inside. "Come in."

Leona entered and gave her a plate covered with a napkin. "Widow said to bring you a biscuit with bacon and honey." She pulled fruit from the pocket of her pants. "Here's an apple. Don't tell her I gave it to ya. She probably won't miss it."

"I'm hungry, thanks. Sit, let's talk. I've got a lot to tell you." She broke off a piece of biscuit and dipped it in honey spread on the edge of the plate.

Leona eyed the black shawl. "Appears expensive."

"Miss Adelaide or one of her people left it on the stoop. My visit with her was successful, she wants me to embroider flowers on it." She lit the kerosene lamp, then poured water from the pitcher into a glass.

"Good, with the extra money you can make a dress that won't cause a ruckus when you go out." She smiled and hesitated before she spoke. "Seen you and Mr. Taylor courtin'."

"What'd you see?" Sarah didn't think anyone could see in her room and she was sure Leona wouldn't be at the creek.

"You sittin' beside him in his buggy heading out of town. Where'd ya go?"

She drank water and ate the bacon. The young girl was naive with the same innocence she'd had until James. Her friend's pretty face hid beneath her scraggly hair and hat and her curves were hidden by the men's clothes she wore. She hoped when Leona's time came, she would find a kind man. "Do you know much about courting and what men and women do if they love each other?"

The girl peered down at her pants and rubbed her hands over her thighs. "I seen a man and woman in the alley one day. He had her pinned against the wall. They were laughin' and kissin'. He pulled her dress up and then he pulled his pants down. His man thing was big, and he put it in her. The lady's eyes were closed but she smiled. I watched, they both enjoyed it, movin' like they wanted to get closer. I thought they were done, but he pulled his thing out and pounded it into her over and over. She moaned and I figured she was hurt but she kept grinning. The woman opened her eyes and caught me starin'. She smiled and winked. I run off. Watchin' them, I felt somethin' down here and I thought I wet my pants." She pointed to her groin. "Is that what goes on at the Social Club? Widow Lowery didn't tell me what went on, but she said I should never go to the Social Club or the saloon. Said respectable women didn't go to those places. If I had a reason, I'd go no matter what the widow says."

She poured water from the pitcher into a bowl and washed her hands. If her mother had explained the birds and bees, would she have let James talk her into it? "When a man and woman love each other, they come together in a mating ritual. It's how women get with child."

Leona said. "Well, I figured that much out by seein' animals, but I never seen a man before, you know, down there. I didn't expect it to be so big. Don't it hurt?"

"There's pain for the woman the first time she lets the man have his way with her, yes." She studied the girl's face to decide how much to share. Her time in bed with James filled her with guilt and regret. He seduced her first by his words, telling her she was too old to be a virgin, and at twenty-one years of age she should know what made her a woman. He toyed with her body while he talked and undressed her. She trembled at his touch and responded with an urge so strong she lost all control. Desperate for release she gave in and let him have his way. The burning pain subsided, and her body tingled on the precipice until he groaned and released in her. He stood and told her to get dressed before someone found them. Her body wanted something she hadn't understood until today with Daniel. She would have that something before she went home. "Promise me you won't get curious but wait until you love someone before you…"

Leona stopped her. "I ain't never doin' it, but I'm glad you told me 'bout it. I been wonderin' on it."

Sarah smiled at her new friend. "Now, tell me what colors would look good as roses on this."

The wash girl studied the hues. "The yellow doesn't work."

Sarah removed the yellow thread and placed it on the table. "The red is good."

"White's no good, needs more color." Leona handed the white thread to Sarah.

She placed the red, pink, and rose thread close together. "These colors remind me of my mother's rose garden at home." She placed several colors of green on the fabric. "And dark green for the vines." She grabbed the white thread. "I'll need a little white for contrast on the roses and gold to mingle in the green leaves."

"Yes, I can imagine the stitching of the colors together." Leona sat in the chair. "Ain't you scared you'll mess up or she won't approve of what you do?"

"I'm apprehensive but not afraid. I've been doing this since I was a young girl." She pointed to the front of the cape. "This shawl just needs a cascade of roses along the front." She pointed to the area.

"The madam is a nice lady. She comes to the dress

shop and always speaks to me if I'm in the store." Leona gazed around the room. "I'll see ya tomorrow."

Sarah hugged her friend. "You're a jewel."

Leona hugged back and grabbed the plate. "Goodnight."

Sarah set up the pattern and prepared the cape for the embroidery. She'd not admitted it, but she was nervous. This needlework had to be perfect. She checked her patterns and colors one more time to make sure. Yes, this was the pattern and the colors blended perfectly with each other. By nightfall she had the shawl ready to start the needlework.

Chapter Eight

After a fitful night of sleep and too much whiskey, Daniel woke at first light with a pain in his head and roiling in his stomach. Sarah stirred up memories of Becca. Memories he should have come to terms with years ago. He had to forgive the woman. Callum had advised him many times that anger at a woman was like a noose around your neck. The more you run, the tighter it gets. Face and forgive. Face and forgive. From now on when memories of Becca infiltrated his world, he would say these words, face his feelings and forgive the woman. It's about damn time, he told himself. The looming concern, the one that had him drinking too much whiskey, was if history would repeat itself. He'd fall for her and she'd leave him. Whatever happened between them, he had to get the memories of Becca out of his mind. Face and forgive, he repeated the mantra as he trimmed his beard and combed his hair. He swallowed a powder for his aching head, ate a cold hard biscuit and washed it down with black coffee before heading to the corral where Callum worked with a stallion. "Going to Holt Ranch and see Caleb about a trade. I told Sarah I'd teach her how to ride and I need a small, calm horse for her."

His friend led the animal to the side of the ring. "Ye be getting serious, then."

"I plan to spend time with her, and every person

61

needs to know how to ride. If he'll trade when will you have this fellow ready?" Callum had seven years on him but sometimes it was as if he were talking to his father.

The trainer rubbed the flank of the quarter horse. "I need to work with him a few more days. He's a beauty with just enough spirit. I think Caleb will approve."

"Fine." He moseyed toward the barn to saddle Kentucky. The Holt ranch wasn't far from his. Caleb Holt had married Laurel Adams and together they raised her son. Envy plagued him every time he visited, although he was delighted for his friend. Caleb was a good man and deserved a family. Laurel was the perfect wife; she'd transformed his ranch into a home with lace curtains and flowers planted in a garden in front of the house. He couldn't be happier for them, but it didn't stop the loneliness that accompanied his solitude. He'd keep his mind on the task. Get a horse for Sarah to ride.

He rode the short distance to the ranch and turned into the lane.

Caleb worked outside the barn bent over a horse's hoof. He placed the animal's foot on the ground before grabbing a rag to wipe his hands. "Daniel, good to see you."

Laurel worked her little garden with her son Jesse, well, Caleb's son now. The boy dug in the dirt with a small shovel. Jealousy doesn't become you, he reminded himself. "Hi, Laurel." He waved.

She stood and stretched her back. "Morning, Daniel."

Kentucky trotted toward the barn with his head raised high. "You damn horse, you should be in a show somewhere," Daniel said under his breath. He dismounted and tied the reins to a post. He approached Caleb and shook his hand. "Good to see you. I need a riding horse for a lady, something small with a calm disposition. Want to talk a trade?"

"Be happy to. I've got a black and white paint, fourteen hands, a Tovero with blue eyes. She's a beauty with a sweet disposition. Come on, I'll show you." He walked into the barn.

Daniel followed him to a stall. The mare stuck her head out and he slipped her a piece of carrot from his pocket. "Hi, girl." He rubbed her head and she nudged him for more treats. "Yes, she'll do fine. I've got a chestnut stallion, sixteen hands. Callum will have him ready in a few days. Want to come by and take a look?"

"No, the Scotsman does good work and you've got the best stock of quarter horses in Wyoming. I'll take the trade. Take her with you and I'll pick mine up by the end of the week." He opened the stall and led the mare from the barn.

Daniel pulled a bridle from his saddlebag and placed it on the horse before tying the reins to his saddle. He mounted Kentucky and turned toward Caleb. "Pleasure doing business with you." He tipped his hat.

"I named her Lady Blue, but you can call her what you want." Caleb waved and headed toward his barn.

"Lady Blue it is." He held Kentucky's reins tight in his hand. "Take it easy and don't show off in front of the lady. Let's get her home safe." Of all the horses he'd owned, Kentucky was the smartest. He swore the animal knew what he was thinking. They made the short ride back to his farm.

Callum met them outside the barn. "Good trade. She be a fine one. I'll get her situated in a stall and rub her down, make the lass feel at home. Got a name?"

"Lady Blue." He dismounted and let Kentucky drink from the trough. "We'll get her settled and I'll ride her tomorrow, want to see how she handles before Sarah rides her. Caleb will come by for the stallion by the end of the week."

The trainer led her into the barn singing, "Lady Blue, the lass with the blue eyes be a good lass, ye be a good lass."

The burley Scottish man tamed the horses with patience. He'd never seen him raise a whip to even the wildest stallion. He'd work months with a charge until he gained their confidence. His singing kept the animals calm, they trusted Callum for their care, and he loved the man like a brother.

After taking care of Kentucky, Daniel entered his house and drank a tonic for his stomach before heading to his office. He did the paperwork for the trade and balanced the books. Business had been good the last few years. The location of his ranch between Cheyenne and Wylder attracted buyers from both towns. He'd seen Wylder grow from a mining village to a good size town. He sent his father the money he gave him to go west although his parents begged him to keep it. Now he saved every dime just in case he met someone to make his bride. He planned to use the money he borrowed for lumber and material to build a new barn. The stock was growing with every pregnant mare and he needed space for the mothers and foals. With the paperwork and books done, he placed his pen and porcelain inkpot to the side of his desk and put the organized papers in a side drawer.

Hard work would eliminate the image of the girl in

town from his mind for a little while. It was time to train one of the male horses to a rider. He found a blanket and saddle from the tack room and placed it in the small pen and ambled to the barn. The young stallion stood in his stall eating oats. He spoke softly to soothe the animal. Out of curiosity the dark brown colt approached. He pulled an apple out of his pocket and cut off pieces with his pocketknife. "Here you go." The stallion ate, and he petted him while he talked quietly. As the horse ate the last bite, he placed the bosal around the animal's nose. He had the hanger around the ears before the horse detected the hackamore. The animal pulled back his head, but Daniel had already completed the task and held the mecate. "Want to go out?" They entered the small arena where he led the horse around the circle several times. The young stallion calmed and followed his orders until he attempted to place the saddle pad on the animal's back. The giant horse reared up and Daniel stepped back out of the way holding the reins but giving the horse space. The animal settled and nodded his head in an attempt to get free. He pulled the mecate tight to show the stallion who was in control and continued to walk him around the arena. He'd trained enough wild horses to know the stallion was close and he'd not give up. Daniel lifted the blanket and softly told the horse his plans. This time the horse pulled away but didn't buck as he placed the pad on his back and continued to guide him around in a circle. Daniel released the reins, picked up the saddle, and placed it on the horse. The animal bucked at having a foreign object placed on his back, but the determined trainer won out. The cinch secured, Daniel mounted the saddle and held the mecate tight as the male horse bucked until he relinquished control to his handler. Daniel guided the horse around the pen teaching commands and giving reinforcement.

Callum stood near a tree watching. Daniel nodded toward his friend, dismounted, and led the young stallion to the fence. "Good job, boy." He murmured to the horse as he lifted the saddle and pad.

The Scotsman approached. "He'll be ready to sell soon."

"He's a beauty and gets along with the others, got a good disposition." Daniel folded the saddle pad over the rail.

"Speaking of temperaments, the paint is a sweet mare." He entered the pen and grabbed the saddle. "If what you say is true, she'll be the perfect horse for Sarah. Never met a woman who didn't ride."

"The girl grew up in a fancy town riding in carriages. The west is foreign. Can't believe she's stayed this long." He led the stallion to the pasture with the other horses. "Going to turn him out and let him graze."

With at least three more hours of sun in the day, Daniel changed clothes and saddled Kentucky for a ride to town. The afternoon was sticky with humidity and dark clouds spotted the western sky. He should put the chores off to another day, but he fancied seeing Sarah and no storm would hinder him. The Sawmill Lumber Company hummed with the sound of men cutting and stacking wood. The smell of dust made him eager to build something. He put in his order and signed a contract agreeing to cash on delivery. They would have the new barn built and ready by the time cold weather set in. His business done, he mounted Kentucky and rode through town to the mercantile.

Finn Wylder greeted him. "Daniel, haven't seen you in a while. How's business on the ranch?"

He shook the owner's hand. "Good, in fact, came to town to order lumber for a new barn."

"Great to hear, success begets success. What can I help you with?" He meandered around the store with Daniel.

"I need a pair of women's riding gloves." He stopped at the display. "Something for a lady with small hands."

Mr. Wylder pulled out a pair made of soft leather. "This is our finest."

Daniel examined them. "Perfect, I'll take 'em." He followed the proprietor to the front and paid. "Pleasure doing business and thanks for the gentleman you sent last month, he left the ranch with a fine mare."

Finn passed his change. "Yes, he came by and showed me. Beautiful animal. You and Callum are making a name for yourselves."

"We enjoy what we do." He nodded and took the gloves.

He left the store and placed his new purchase in the saddle bag, pulled the horse's face toward his and murmured, "I'll be back soon." Kentucky nodded his head and whinnied. Daniel made his way around the corner toward the dress shop always on alert for the Nelson brothers. Mildred Lowery stood in the window and he tipped his hat. The woman waved and if he didn't know otherwise, a slight smile teased her face. He ascended the steps to Sarah's room. He knocked on the door and searched the street for danger.

"Daniel." She allowed him entrance.

"I had some errands to run in town and wanted to say hello. Have you eaten supper?" He pulled her toward him, his arms wrapped around her small body. She tiptoed and lifted her face to him ready for a kiss. His unabated lust drove the kiss as he devoured her luscious mouth. He parted her lips with his tongue, she whimpered and opened to him, the sensation so strong it stoked the internal fire in his belly. He wanted, damn he wanted her not for this moment, not to satisfy his carnal desire, he wanted her for always. He drew on all things holy to retain his good judgment. A deep breath filled his lungs and he steadied her against him while he inhaled the scent of a spring flower garden with her usual lilac scent and a hint of rose. "Get your hat."

"Give me just a minute." She tipped the pitcher, poured water on a cloth, and washed her face. A glance in the mirror and the ribbons from the hat secured under her chin, she turned and presented him with a flirty grin. "I'm ready."

Sarah bounded down the stairs in front of him. When they entered the street, he took her hand and threaded it through his bent arm. He kept his other hand free, ready to pull his revolver if necessary. He inspected the sides of the buildings, alleys, and benches but found no sign of the Nelsons. They entered the Vincent House Hotel and made their way to the restaurant. A waiter led them to a table for two.

"This has become my favorite place," she said as she perused the menu.

"How's your job?" He placed a napkin in his lap.

"I am grateful for it. Jake's a fine boss, Miss Adelaide, too. When I arrived, I had nothing and now I have two jobs." She placed her menu on the table and smiled at a man across the room.

"He comes in for breakfast every day." She rolled her eyes toward the man.

"That's Mr. McCabe from the law office." He nodded and smiled at the lawyer. "Did you have a job in Savannah?"

"Heavens, no." She placed her reticule on the table and unfolded her napkin before placing it in her lap. "Papa would never allow it. I have to say, I'm enjoying this adventure except for the gunshots at night and men trying to attack me."

He held her hand in his. "I wish I could protect you. I want you to be careful and aware of who's around you at all times."

"I'm learning as I go, and that lesson I learned the first day." She drew her hand back as the waiter approached.

He ordered for them and chuckled as the ravenous little woman ate. He ordered two small glasses of brandy for a digestif. "Here's to us." He raised his glass and clinked with hers.

She looked at him over the top of her glass and smiled. He nodded; his gaze drifted to her neck. An urge to lean over the table and kiss her tender skin nudged him forward but the room full of people enjoying their afternoon meal stopped him. "Your work at Jake's Place must be tiring."

She put the small glass on the table. "Standing on my feet all day and serving is hard work but I enjoy being there. The customers talk to me and tell me lots of secrets."

"Like what?" He took her hand in his.

She leaned forward and whispered. "I can't tell

you."

He released her hand and leaned back in his chair. "You've been in Wylder long enough to know there are no secrets in this town, especially if your aunt finds out. They must really trust you to confide in you knowing you could spread gossip as soon as they walk out the door."

"Sometimes I think they want the information known." She swallowed another sip of brandy.

Daniel paid the bill and escorted Sarah out of the hotel. As they stepped outside, he noticed the swirling clouds above. A storm brewed with thunder and lightning in the distance. They hurried to her rented room and he stood at the top of the stairs and studied the streets for miscreants. "I wanted to stay and take a walk around town but looks like I won't make it home before the rain hits." He took her hand, removed her glove, and brushed his lips over her knuckles.

She gave him a chaste kiss on his cheek. "Thank you for my meal. Be safe on your way home."

He extended his arm to motion her inside. He waited until he heard the lock click and the slide of the chair before he bolted down the stairs to his horse. Kentucky sensed his approach and lifted his head in a loud neigh. He petted the animal before he untied the reins. "Time to go home, boy." Daniel put his foot in the stirrup, swung his body over the horse and took off out of town driving the horse to a fast gallop. He smelled the rain before it arrived. A deluge soaked him and Kentucky. The loud thunder spurred the horse to a gallop so fast he had to pull the reins back in order to regain control of the speed. The horse's hooves brought mud from the earth to cover his pants with muck. The lane to his house was a welcome sight and he guided Kentucky straight to the barn.

Callum stood just inside the structure and took the reins. "Did you get your business done?"

Daniel took his hat off and shook the water from the Stetson. "Lumber will be delivered as soon as it's measured and cut. Next spring we'll have room for all the mares and their offspring."

"Did you see the lass?" Callum wiped mud from Kentucky's flank.

"Had a meal with her. She's thriving with her job, making friends." He assisted Callum with the animal. "Don't expect her to stay past autumn."

Callum led Kentucky to his stall. "I believe her leaving or staying is up to you."

He headed to his house to get dry clothes. Callum's words played in his mind. The girl already made up her mind when she got off the train. She'd go back, just like every other fine lady he'd known.

Chapter Nine

Sarah balanced three plates in her hands as she walked into the dining room. Her gaze flew to the table by the window and her stomach took a tumble. The Nelson brothers sat together waiting for food. She prayed they had left town but here they were, and she had to be nice and serve them. She placed the order in front of the three gentleman diners and walked through the crowded restaurant toward the table to take the brothers' order.

Jasper recognized her and banged a fist on the table. "We need coffee."

She grabbed two cups, the pot and approached their table. She poured the strong black liquid in the mugs. "I'll have your breakfast out in a few moments."

"Not so fast." Jasper grabbed her arm. "I ain't forgot what you did to me," he growled in a low voice. "You'll regret that little move next time I get you alone."

She struggled to free her arm from his grasp, the more she resisted, the more her arm burned. Anger slammed through her, she wanted to pour the hot liquid from the pot over his head. Instead, she responded in a carefully controlled tone. "You'll never get me alone." Her teeth ground together. "Take your hands off me."

He released her and the blood traveled through the veins of her arm.

Jasper stretched his leg to keep her pinned at their table. "Spunky and purdy. Ain't she purdy, Silus."

"Purdy as a picture." The brother put his hand on her back side. "Now this is a better dress. Never cared for pads covering a woman's ass."

She stepped over the outstretched leg. The other customers stared with interest. A man she didn't know rose, his hand hovering near his side arm.

Jasper put his hands in front of him. "No need, friend. We were just havin' a little fun with the lady."

The man eyed him with disgust and sat down.

Sarah's body trembled with fear as she hurried into the kitchen. "Two more plates."

Jake lurched from the stove and helped her into a chair. "What happened, you all right? Did you drop a plate? Told you not to carry so many."

She exhaled. "The Nelson brothers are in the dining room. I had a confrontation with them the day I arrived. They scare me."

He handed her a cup of water. "I know 'em. Nothin' but trouble. I can throw 'em out."

"No, that will make it worse. Some man stood up for me and they stopped bothering me." She took a sip of the water. "Let's just serve them and let them be on their way."

He piled the plates high with scrambled eggs, fried potatoes and onions, slices of ham and cathead biscuits. "I'll take these out."

Sarah followed him with the coffee pot, filling empty cups along the way. Jake placed the plates on the table and leaned down. What he said to the brothers, she didn't know, but they nodded their head and ate breakfast like starving wolves. She moved to their table and refilled their cups without incident.

Busy with other customers, she didn't see them leave. As she cleared the table, she dropped their money in the pocket sewed into her apron. So they were back in town. The danger of her situation caused her hair to lift on the back of her neck. Her legs rooted to the floor and she gripped the plates until a man demanded she take his order. "Be right there." Sarah deposited the plates on the sideboard and forced her attention back to her work.

The last breakfast customer left the restaurant. Sarah tidied up the tables and adjusted the chairs for the afternoon rush. Jake had placed the freshly washed knives, spoons, and forks on the sideboard. She readied the tableware and napkins for easy access because once the crowd arrived, she had no time to spare. She'd learned that the first day. "Think ahead," Jake advised her the morning he hired her. When the dining room was to her liking, she entered the kitchen ready for a cooking lesson. She enjoyed learning the new art and tasks of cookery. He'd promised her a lesson in preparing mashed potatoes.

"Don't take off too much skin, you'll waste the potato if you do." He instructed when he'd checked her first two potatoes and found most of the tuber in the waste bucket. She loved the feel of the spud in her hands and wanted to learn the process of cooking the hard vegetable into a fluffy delight.

She found she loved working with her hands, turning the raw ingredients into a delicious masterpiece just as she did her embroidery. "I never cooked before. Mother always had a woman who prepared meals for the family."

"Unless you marry a wealthy man, which there aren't any in this town, you'll need to know how to cook. When you're done with the potatoes, we'll start on the onions." He put a basket of large onions on the table.

She peeled the outer layer of the round vegetable and placed them in a bowl.

He grabbed one. "We're gonna cut these in large pieces to cook in the squash. The juice from the onion may make you cry, it's normal."

She focused on his technique and sliced her onion in pieces to match his. Her eyes stung and tears dripped down her face. The more she worked the stronger the assault. Her eyes closed voluntarily, and she struggled to keep them open. She raised her hand to her face to wipe the tears.

He put his hand on her arm. "Don't touch your eye, just makes the pain worse. As soon as you're done, wash your hands and dry your face with a rag."

As she worked, she grew used to the smell and the tears subsided. She sauntered to the stove as he stirred the pot of potatoes.

Jake handed her a small knife. "Stick this in a potato, if the tip goes in easily and the potato slips off when you hold up the knife, then they're done."

She inserted the knife, the vegetable slipped off and fell back into the pan of boiling water. "I think they're ready."

He spooned the potatoes into a huge bowl. "Get the crock of butter and pitcher of milk." He mashed the potatoes with a large wooden spoon. "Pour some milk to the side of the dish and give me a good knob of the shortening."

She observed his technique and filed the instructions in her memory, adding more ingredients as he requested. "So that's how they get fluffy. You make the best I've ever tasted."

"Hand me the box of salt on the shelf." He poured salt in his hand and sprinkled it over the creamed potatoes. "You stir." He handed her the spoon. "Go deep and mix from the bottom so all the potatoes have flavor blended in."

She moved the spoon through the large bowl of potatoes. "How do you know how much of each ingredient to add?"

He scooped the fluffy mixture on a fork. "Check for salt, butter and creaminess. If more seasoning is needed, now's the time to adjust. Cooking is practice, tasting, and patience."

She savored the flavors of each ingredient. "I think all they need are eating. They're wonderful."

"People will be coming in soon. If they ask, we're having roasted pork, creamed potatoes, squash and onions, and hoecakes. Dessert is apple cobbler." He glanced at his waitress. "Better comb your hair."

She gazed in the mirror mounted on the wall and smoothed her coiffure. The wood stove made the heat in the kitchen almost unbearable and her dress was moist with perspiration. "I'll check all the tables and make sure the dining room is set."

The last customer left the café and Jake locked the door. After he put the chairs on the tables, Sarah swept the floor and scooped up breadcrumbs and dirt to deposit in the trash can. Jake left her in charge of the dining room while he cleaned the kitchen area. Her back ached from the long day on her feet, she stretched to release the tension in her neck and spine and set her mind to her last chore. She sorted the tableware Jake had washed and left for her on the sideboard and separated the knives, forks, and spoons in readiness for the breakfast rush. One last glance around the space and a tired satisfaction settled over her. She opened the door to the kitchen. "I'll see you in the morning, Jake."

Jake stood with a mop in his hand ready to clean the dining room floor. "Thanks. Have a good evening."

Sarah searched the area before stepping out into the street. The Nelson brothers leaned against a post in front of the Longhorn Saloon. Silus saw her first and elbowed his brother. Jasper threw his smoke down and they ambled toward the café.

Fear vibrated through her bones causing her legs to buckle. She slammed the door and hurried to the kitchen. "Jasper and Silus are out there. I'm afraid to cross the street."

Jake grabbed the shotgun in the corner. "I'll see you get home." He stepped outside and stood on the wooden porch, his gun at his side.

The men slithered toward the stairs leading to Sarah's room. They both grinned at her as they passed the dress shop.

She stood with Jake until they were out of sight. "Guess I'll be on my way. Thanks for protecting me."

"You be careful, they ain't nothin' but no-goods." He waited while she climbed the steps.

She made it to the top of the stairs without incident and waved at Jake. "See you in the morning."

Sarah fell in the straight chair and put her head in her hands. She'd begun to feel comfortable in the town, obtaining work, meeting nice people, making friends, but couldn't shake the unpleasant vibration of hatred from the Nelsons. What could make a man deliberately hurt another? Her mind shifted to James, he'd hurt her mentally, taking her virginity and disappearing into the night. These men were more dangerous because they would hurt her physically and given the chance, they would take everything James took and more.

****

Saturday morning Sarah rose early eager to spend the day on her needlework. After a quick breakfast of left-over biscuits from Jake she stood at the washstand and performed her toilette. She preferred a soak in the washtub, but she'd become adept at the art of using the water pitcher and bowl. A few drops of lilac oil in the water and the new soap she found at the mercantile were sufficient. She stepped into a clean dress, fastened the buttons, and combed her hair, finally ready to spend the morning on embroidery.

The right side of the cape was almost finished. The cascade of roses in red, rose, and pink flowed from the top of the garment to two inches above the hem. While working she contemplated leaving, returning home to Savannah. One more week of work on the cape and she'd be done. The Nelson Brothers would be a story she could tell her friends about. They'd laugh about her kneeing him and running away, and they'd congratulate her on her bravery. Home was just a train ticket away. Facing the gossip from the biddies in Savannah was nothing compared to the terror she faced walking down the streets of Wylder. A knock on her door sent a wave of fear through her stomach. She peeked through a slit in the curtain and opened the door.

Chapter Ten

Daniel parked the small buggy in front of the dress shop and scurried up the stairs to Sarah's room. He knocked and searched the street. The curtain swayed and his girl peeped around the blue and white checked fabric.

She opened the door and greeted him. "Hi, I didn't expect to see you today."

He stepped inside and closed the door. "Mighty fine needlework you're doing."

She held the cape in front of her. "It's not for me, this is what I've been working on for Miss Adelaide. You really think it's good?"

He admired the stitchery. "This is a work of art. Never seen such fine embroidery."

"I enjoy working with my hands. This will keep me busy when I'm not working at Jake's. Idle hands and all that, you know." She carefully placed the shawl on the bed. "What do I owe this surprise visit?"

He pulled her in his arms and kissed her, then placed his hand under her chin and raised her head. "Wanted to see you, make sure you made it through the week." She tiptoed and placed her arms around his neck, then she kissed him. He groaned and held her body tight against his. She opened her mouth to his passion. He explored, setting to memory the taste, smell and feel of this woman. He couldn't get enough of her, would never be able to get enough. He claimed her lips for a long time until he figured he'd either have to stop or take her to bed. "Want to ride out to the ranch with me?"

She steadied herself against him. "I'd love to see your ranch. Let me get my bonnet."

He spotted the straw head covering on the table. "Happy to see you have a practical hat."

She placed it on her head and tied the ribbons. "I had enough money to buy something extra and my nice millinery is becoming filthy. The dirt from the streets and cattle herded through town create a constant cloud of dust."

He tilted her head and smiled. "You look adorable. After you." With the door secure, he pushed away the notion that if anyone wanted to, they could easily smash their way in.

"I've got a surprise for you." Daniel assisted her into his carriage. He chuckled as she squirmed in her seat and watched him walk around the rear of the buggy. The carriage sank under his weight as he stepped into his seat. "I'm not telling you."

She put her hands in her lap and sat straighter. "Why not?"

"It's a surprise. I can tell you don't enjoy surprises and you're probably the type girl who always gets her way." He guided the carriage toward the road to the ranch. He'd taken another quarter horse today, Kentucky waited at the ranch with Lady Blue. "Tell me about your week."

"I'm learning to cook. Jake is teaching me."

He glanced toward her. "You don't know how to prepare a meal?"

She gave him a firm stare. "We had a cook. Did you know how to before you came west?"

"Guess you've got a point." Eager to get her to his place, he flung the reins and yelled, "Yeehaw." The quarter horse picked up his pace.

She fidgeted with her drawstring bag. "Oh, and the Nelson's came in the restaurant for breakfast one day."

He kept his eyes on the road. "Any trouble?"

"They cornered me, but a gentleman stood and put his hand on his sidearm. They backed off and Jake said something to them as he set their plates on the table. They ate quickly and left." Her voice trailed off.

He turned and looked at her. She would be helpless against these men and there was not a damn thing he could do about it. "What else? Did you run into them after that?"

She sucked in a breath and exhaled a sigh. "Yes, they were outside the restaurant when I walked home, so Jake stood at the door with his shotgun to see me to my room."

Son of a bitch, the sorry bastards. He would never take another's life, but these men were causing him to question his morality. "I hope you're careful when you go out and always lock up. Keep placing the chair in front of the door." He slowed the buggy as they got closer.

"They scare me." She put her hand on his thigh.

Her touch scorched his leg and sent a jolt first to his groin and then his heart. If these men hurt her, or any man for that matter, he'd kill every damn one of them. "If they bother you or anyone bothers you, you head straight for the sheriff and if you can't, scream as loud as you can. Will you do that?"

"Yes."

She squeezed his leg tighter. He wanted to bring her to the ranch and let her live in his house, but she was in Wylder because of her reputation back home. He wouldn't risk the damage to her character. As if anyone in Wylder cared a hoot. He turned onto the lane to his house. "This is the LT." He said with pride.

She read the sign over the archway. "Lex Taylor Ranch. Is that your house?"

"Yes, you like?" The large two-story loomed ahead of them.

"It's beautiful." She folded her hands under her chin. "I never expected to see such a fine house in the west."

"It's a replica of the home my parents have in Lexington, on a smaller scale, of course. You've only seen Wylder, I'll take you to Cheyenne one day. It's a big town with a more reputable population and fine stores." He pulled the buggy in front of the house. "Do you want to see the inside, or do you want your surprise?"

She jumped up. "Surprise."

"Sit and I'll drive us to the barn."

Callum came out of the stalls and took charge of the horse and buggy. "Top of the day, Sarah."

"Hello." She jumped from the buggy before Daniel could help her.

The horseman winked at his boss. "Got everything ready for ye."

He guided Sarah into the barn where Kentucky and the new mare were saddled and ready to ride. "I bought you a horse."

"You bought me a horse?" Her forehead creased. "I

82

mean, you bought me a horse, how considerate of you." She stared at the large animals who stuck their heads from the stalls.

"Come and meet Lady Blue." He grabbed her hand and tugged her toward the mare. "She's very gentle, perfect for you to learn how to ride." He placed Sarah's hand on the animal's head. She pulled her hand away and shrank back. He remembered the girl had never ridden a horse or taken care of one for that matter. "There's nothing to be afraid of, she's gentle." He extracted a piece of carrot from his pocket. "Give this to the mare."

Sarah held the vegetable with her thumb and forefinger.

He took the piece of carrot. "Put it in the palm of your hand and hold it in front of her." He presented the vegetable. The mare took the carrot from his hand and chomped down.

"Give me one, let me try." She did the same and Lady Blue ate the treat and nudged her head against Sarah's arm.

"Appears she likes you." He whispered in the animal's ear. "Lady Blue, this is Sarah. She's your new best friend." The horse moved closer in search of more food.

Sarah rubbed the mare's head. "She is sweet." She inspected the horse's face. "I didn't know horses had blue eyes."

"It's a trait common with toveros." Pride welled in his chest as he watched his girl take to the horse. "I've seen some with one blue eye and one brown eye."

"She's beautiful." A smile danced on her lips. "Do you think she'll let me ride her?"

"I was hoping you'd say that." Their conversation was interrupted when Kentucky pounded his hoof on the barn floor. Daniel walked to the quarter horse's stall. "I see you, show-off. Calm down, I'll be back for you later." He led Lady Blue from her stall. "Let's go to the corral and get you in the saddle. Walk beside me, don't get behind, she might get scared and kick.

"You've never been on a horse, am I correct?" As they walked, he examined the ground for any horse manure they would need to step over.

"Never." She eased close beside him. "I'm a little nervous."

"Try not to be, because Lady Blue will know." They paused at the gate to the arena and he removed her gloves from his pocket. "Put these on to protect your hands."

Sarah rubbed the soft leather against her cheek. "These are beautiful, so soft. Thank you."

He held her hands out and admired the leather. "Perfect fit."

He lifted the latch and pushed the door. "Go in and stand by the fence."

Daniel guided the mare into the ring and addressed Sarah. "Come forward and stand beside me." She gave him a frightened look but moved forward. He turned her head up and gazed in her eyes. "Don't be afraid."

She rubbed Lady Blue's side. "I don't even know how to get on her."

Daniel checked the cinches on the saddle. "It's easy. I'll hold the reins while you mount her."

She eyed the saddle and then him. "How?"

"Let me show you. Put your left foot in the stirrup and swing yourself into the saddle." He swung onto the horse and Lady Blue pranced a bit. "Take hold of the reins to steady her but don't force her." He slipped from the saddle to the ground.

She held the saddle horn and placed her foot in the stirrup and tried. "I can't."

"Try again." Daniel waited until her foot was in the stirrup and lifted her body to the saddle. Her dress rose above her ankles and he chuckled at the ruffles of white that hid her legs. "Your pretty lace pantaloons are gonna get mighty dirty."

She tugged her dress, but the material didn't cover the bloomers. "Leona can get them clean. What do I do now?"

"I'll hold the reins and walk her around the arena so the two of you can get used to each other." He quickened the pace when he was confident both the horse and rider were comfortable. After a couple of rounds, he stopped and handed the reins to Sarah. "Hold the straps, use them to guide her where you want to go. To stop, tighten the hold. Let her know you're the boss, be kind and this mare will take care of you. Go around by yourself a few times and we'll go for a ride."

Daniel sat tall on the fence; a satisfied grin covered his face and pride swelled in his chest. His gentlewoman rode a horse as if she were born to it. Her body rose and fell in the saddle with the rhythm of the horse's gait. Caleb was right, Lady Blue was the perfect horse for a woman. He jumped from the fence and stopped Sarah on her next round. He took the reins, tied the leather straps to the fence, and helped her off the horse. "Wait here and I'll get Kentucky." Sarah ran her hand over the horse's neck, petting and talking softly. He smiled. No prettier sight in all the world.

They rode toward the pasture where the quarter horses grazed. He kept Kentucky at a slow trot and Lady Blue followed suit. The stallion strutted and pranced about, leading the mare through the field. They stopped at the fence where he dismounted and tied the reins. He reached for her. "Let's walk around, you can get sore if you aren't used to riding."

With his help, she slid to the ground rubbing her back side. "I think I'm already sore. Do all these belong to you?"

"They do." He put a foot on the rail and leaned on the fence. "Keeps Callum and me busy. He's the best horse trainer I've ever met." One of the stallions ambled over, curious of the new mare.

She touched the horse's forehead. "Do you get lonely isolated as you are from town?"

"You get used to solitude." He removed her hat, kissed her, and held her in his arms. He had everything he ever wanted or needed right in front of him. His animals, his land, his woman. How long would she remain in Wylder? Would she up and leave without telling him? *Don't dwell on the negative.* "Let's head back. Want to show you the house."

Chapter Eleven

Daniel and Callum led the horses to their stalls and removed the saddle, bridle, and pad. The Scotsman took care of Kentucky while Daniel settled Lady Blue. Sarah sat on an overturned bucket and watched her cowboy rub the horse's legs and brush her coat. She fell in love with the animal after discovering what a kind soul the mare had and looked forward to more horseback rides with Daniel. Riding through the meadows on Lady Blue, she experienced freedom for the first time in her life. Not once did she think of James, her parents, Silus and Jasper, or her difficult life in Wylder. "You should let me do something." She stood and walked to Lady Blue's stall yearning to feel connection to the animal again. The horse wandered toward her seeking the same. Sarah rubbed the mare's neck and gazed into the animal's blue eyes.

Daniel smiled and continued his work. "Watch and learn. Next time I'll let you take care of your horse."

Yes, there will be a next time. This had been the best day of her life.

Daniel held her small hand in his as they walked from the stalls. "You rode Lady Blue as if you'd done it all your life."

"You're a good teacher." No one could bother her on his ranch. He wouldn't let them. She reveled in the awareness.

Daniel's stately house stood like a castle in the wilderness. The home rivaled the mansions in Savannah. It had a large front porch at the entrance and another front porch on the upper level. Rocking chairs occupied both verandas. "Your home is beautiful."

She walked inside. Dark wood floors met her in the foyer with a large staircase leading to the second floor. A rug runner in deep crimson and blue covered the middle of the steps.

He led her to a large room on the right of the stairs. "This is my office and library."

A large mahogany desk and chair sat in the corner. He'd positioned a green velvet settee before the fireplace with a small table to the side laden with books. A ledger lay open on the desk. A man's room, even smelled of him, leather and soap. A scent she'd come to love. A side table held his bourbon and several glasses. The bookshelves covered the wall from floor to ceiling and a small ladder nestled in the corner. "You stay in this room most of the time?"

"Yes, this is where I get most of the work of the ranch done."

Sarah followed him from room to room. Each space was beautifully decorated. She held the rail as they ascended the stairs, her legs unsteady in anticipation of seeing his bedroom. Their footsteps echoed through the space at the top of the stairs which led to four rooms. He took her hand and opened the door to a large bedroom. The afternoon sun beamed through the curtains making the room bright compared to the stairs and hallway. The dark wood four poster bed sat in the middle of the room. Along the wall were cabinets and a dressing table. The fireplace had wood stacked, ready for winter.

She wanted to say something, tell him how lovely everything looked. How he'd done a wonderful job with his house and furnishings. She turned to tell him, but his gaze stopped her. His look seared her soul with desire and beckoned her toward him. As if she traveled through time and space, she found his embrace.

Daniel held her close and rested his chin on the top of her head. "I don't know how we found each other, but I'm glad we did." He turned her face up and claimed her lips.

The fiery kiss stirred a passion that bloomed in her belly and raced through her blood. He stopped kissing her and she inhaled a deep breath. The smell of leather and everything Daniel fanned the flames. She wanted this man and he wanted her. She closed her eyes and bit her bottom lip. Would he think she an immoral woman if she let him love her?

He put his fingers under her chin and tugged her face up. "Are you all right?"

The tenderness she found in his eyes answered her question. "I am." She placed her hands around his neck and pulled his face to hers. She kissed him, opening her mouth to his sensual kiss. She followed his lead as he waltzed her around the room. He held her close while his fingers gently caressed her body, and his mouth did wonderful things to her lips. They stopped beside the bed and he held her at arm's length. She reached for the lace on his shirt and untied the strings.

He pulled off the shirt and threw it on a chair. He gazed down. "Sarah, I want you. I need you more than I've ever needed a woman, but if you don't want this, say so now."

She rested her hands on the chiseled muscles of his chest. "I want this." At her words, her body readied itself. Moisture wept from her core and his touch sent waves of desire causing her breasts to ache.

He unbuttoned her dress and let the garment fall to the floor. She stood before him in her chemise and pantaloons. He seated her on the bed and removed her shoes and stockings before he shed his boots and pants.

Sarah's blood pumped a tingling sensation through her entire body as she watched him undress, his desire for her evident by the straining fabric of his underpants.

He joined her on the bed and pulled her close while their lips met in a hungry kiss. He tugged her chemise over her head and ran a finger over her nipple. Her breath caught and her center contracted. James had never done anything more than kiss her before he took her. She had no idea her breasts could ignite such a fire in her belly. He sucked her nipple while teasing the other. She inhaled jagged breaths; her whole being floated as if gravity didn't exist. He positioned her on the pillows and removed her bloomers, then stripped off his remaining clothes.

He spread her legs apart and kissed her mound. A whimper escaped her lips and an acceleration of urgency caused her to raise her hips. The embarrassment of what they were doing fled when she cried out in release. He pulled her to his side and held her, kissed her, and teased her nipple with his thumb. His erection burned her leg and she craved him. Desperate with need she whispered. "Daniel, please."

He stopped kissing her, their foreheads touched. "Please what, Sarah?"

She sucked in a breath, this one deep and sure.

"Make love to me."

He placed her on her back and rose over her.

She readied her body for the barrage. A fullness entered her core but no pain as it had been with James. Sarah stared into Daniel's eyes as he loved her so tenderly a tear dripped from her eye. A rising sensation sparked inside her belly and she wanted more. She moved her hips and met his thrusts. His face bore the ecstasy of their coupling as he quickened the pace. Another wave lifted her, and she rode it with him, eyes closed, greedy for her release.

Daniel called out her name, groaned, and spilled his seed inside her womb. The wave crested and she cried out as the release took her. God in Heaven, the tingling would not stop, nor did she want it to.

Daniel rolled them to their sides and cradled Sarah in his arms. He settled her hair away from her face. "You are the most beautiful woman I've ever known. So sweet and perfect."

She ran her hands over his chest admiring his sun-tanned skin. "You are a handsome man, Daniel Taylor."

The fading light in the bedroom reminded her the day would end soon. "Guess you better take me back to town."

He pulled her up from the bed and dressed her before donning his clothes. "I've got biscuits and beef roast and gravy in the kitchen."

Sarah followed him and helped carry the food and drink to the dining room table. No words were spoken while they ate but he smiled and winked a couple of times. Her face reddened as the realization of the afternoon dawned on her.

Daniel put his fork on his plate and reached for her

hand. He brought it to his lips and graced it with a kiss. "Sarah, don't be shy. I don't know how it was with you and your fiancé but what we did today was from my heart. I'm falling in love with you, sweetheart."

No one had ever referred to her with an endearment. If her heart grew any bigger it would smother her lungs. "No, nothing like this."

As the carriage drew closer to the streets of Wylder, the sun settled near the horizon, causing the clouds to turn an orange color against the blue of the sky. "The sunsets in Wyoming are more beautiful than the sun setting on the Atlantic Ocean," Sarah said, gazing into the open sky.

"I think so." Daniel slowed the horse and stopped so they could watch the sun as it drifted lower.

She placed her hand on his, aware that she'd never been this forward with a man. She spoke softly. "I hope you don't think I'm a wanton woman."

He shook his head and touched her face. "No, Sarah. You are a good, kind, and decent gentlewoman. What happened between us was exactly what takes place between a woman and man in love."

She watched the sky change colors and pondered his words. Her life changed its course today. Daniel taught her more than how to ride a horse. He taught her how to be a woman.

Chapter Twelve

Daniel and Callum moseyed through the streets of Cheyenne. People from all around the territory milled about, in search of a horse, mule, or donkey at a good price. Most of the sellers were reputable but there were some shysters trying to make money swindling the public with stolen or unhealthy animals. Daniel sauntered toward the makeshift stables and stopped when he realized Callum was not with him. He turned. His friend stood like a tree and watched a red-haired woman enter a fancy buggy with a man. Callum tipped his hat toward the woman. The lady gave the Scotsman a sly grin. He waited for his friend to catch up. "The redhead catch your eye?"

"Aye, she did. A lovely lass, she is." Callum stared at the back of the buggy.

"Careful, she's got a man." He hadn't seen his friend lust after just one woman. The man loved all women. "You'll forget about her next time you're at the whorehouse."

"She's the best looking one I've seen in five years. Besides, he's old enough to be her father." He reached for Daniel's arm, the men stopped and faced each other. "If the rumor I hear is true, they've got a Clydesdale for sale. If you don't mind, I want to buy the animal and raise drafts on the ranch. Wanted to get your approval first."

Callum admired the huge animals; they were all he talked about when he arrived in Kentucky. "I'm seeing a demand for the stock. Sure, don't see a problem." Since his rendezvous with Sarah, his vision of what he wanted his world to be became clear. He wanted her beside him, as his wife, his lover, his friend, and his partner. Before her, he did his job to make money and prove to his family he could be successful on his own. Now, she mattered most. What she perceived of him, his success, even his failures, he wanted everything to be for her, for their family. Callum was family and his happiness mattered, also.

"Would be nice if they had a mare and stallion for breeding but buy what they have, we'll figure it out as we go. I've had inquiries about drafts, they're strong and make for good work horses, clearing land and pulling logs." They pushed their way through the crowd to the livery. Animals lined the street with owners standing nearby to answer questions. "I'll see to the quarter horses. You check out your Clydesdale before someone buys it."

Daniel pushed through the crowd and spotted a chestnut mare. Everyone was watching a spirited stallion as the owner tugged at the reins to settle the wild steed. No one paid any attention to the female quarter horse. He approached the owner who curried the coat. "Afternoon."

The man stopped his work. "You interested in a mare? Most people goin' for the wild fellow over there."

He glanced at the crowd. "Don't think they want to buy him, just want to see him put on a show. Wouldn't know what to do with him if they had him."

The owner put his brush down and extended his hand. "Jim Tanner. Ah, they wouldn't, but I get the impression you would."

He shook the man's hand. "I know a little, but I've got a Scotsman who works for me, he's a master trainer. You've got what I'm looking for. I've a little ranch in Wylder, The Lex Taylor Ranch."

"Yeah, I've heard of you. You've a good reputation." The old man held the horse's head while Daniel inspected her mouth. "She's a good one. Three years and fifteen hands."

He meandered around checking the hoofs and legs. No signs of abuse, the mare had been well taken care of. "Did you raise her?"

"Sure did, I have a small place east of Cheyenne, not as big as you but it's an income."

"I'll take her." He followed the owner to the tables set up for the sale and they made a deal. He handed over the money and Mr. Tanner filled out the paperwork.

Daniel led his new quarter horse down the street. Callum stood at the entrance to an alleyway holding the reins of a draft horse. The animal was dark brown with white on all four legs. Callum grinned like a boy with his first piece of candy. "An impressive stallion."

"Aye, this stud is the beginning of my Clydesdale endeavor. The gent says he'll search for a mare for me. This beauty is named Icefall because of the white feather on his legs. He's nineteen hands and a gentler steed ye'll never find. We've been talking to each other while we waited. Appears ye got yerself a fine filly."

"Yes, bought her from Jim Tanner. You know him?"

"Aye, he's a good man. Met him last time I came to Cheyenne, played a game of poker with him. If you'd leave the ranch more often, you'd meet people."

"I don't care about gambling and women and there isn't much else to do." Until now, he discerned.

The men tied the reins of the new horses to their saddle horns. Kentucky nudged the mare with interest, and she shied away. "Playing hard to get, eh?" Daniel petted the mare before he climbed in the saddle and guided Kentucky forward. He cracked a few jokes with Callum about the red-haired woman. If he didn't know better, he thought he detected sadness from the Scotsman when they left the city. Callum seemed on high alert, searching the streets before they departed Cheyenne. They arrived at the ranch and settled the new purchases in their respective stalls. First, they unsaddled and cared for Kentucky and Finlay then turned their attention to the newly purchased animals. Daniel fed and watered the mare and filled a bucket with oats.

He grabbed a curry comb and entered Icefall's stall. "Fine stock, this one." He brushed one side of the animal's body while Callum worked on the other. The draft enjoyed the attention and nudged his arm. He ran his hand over the horse's face. "You're a fine fellow, Icefall." The stallion threw his head up and whinnied.

"Smart, too." Callum beamed like a proud father.

The chores done; the men went their separate ways to their abodes. "See you in the morning." Daniel called after his friend.

"Aye, that ye will." Callum strolled toward his small ranch house.

****

96

Daniel poured a finger of his fine Kentucky whiskey, placed the bottle on the table beside his favorite chair, and sat. The clock on the mantel chimed seven in the evening. Sarah would be in her room doing her fancy stitching for one of the ladies from the social club. He knocked the liquid back and contemplated his next move. He'd bedded her and the memory kept him hard most of the time. He'd tempered his wants for the last few years with distractions from manual labor with his horses and the paperwork needed to run the ranch. The distractions hadn't worked with Sarah, only Kentucky mash dulled the desire. He didn't feel guilty about their tryst, she admitted she wanted to as much as he did. The dull pain in his gut and his growing dependence on alcohol grew from his uneasiness that one day he'd ride into town to see her and find her gone. He wouldn't give up hope and he wouldn't stop bedding her if she was willing. She had ingrained herself so deeply into him he recognized his life would never be the same with or without her.

Chapter Thirteen

Sarah stood on a stool in Lowery's Dress Shoppe while Laurel Holt took her measurements for a new work dress. Her feet ached after standing on her feet all day at Jake's Place, and she shifted her weight from one foot to the other.

Laurel wrote down measurements on a piece of paper. "Do you need to sit down?"

"No, I'm fine, just tired from work." She focused her gaze on Jesse, Laurel's son who sat nearby playing with a wooden horse. She stood still and stared at the boy while Laurel measured her from shoulder to ankle. "He's a very good child."

"He grew up beside me while I worked. I taught him from a baby to mind me and let me take care of my business. He gets a little rambunctious at times but that's the boy coming out in him." Laurel extended her hand and helped Sarah off the stool. "How soon do you need this?"

She perused several stacks of fabric until she found the material she wanted. "At your convenience. I have a dress I wear, just needed another." She passed the bolt of fabric to Mildred.

"You own one plain dress, and you work at Jake's Place every day? Your dress will be worn out from washing. I can make two as easily as one. Choose another fabric and I'll have both for you by the end of the week."

Sarah calculated the price for the supplies and Laurel's fee in her head. With the money from her job and the work the madam promised, she'd have enough. The way she was going, she'd return home with more money than when she arrived in Wylder. "Yes, two dresses and I could use another apron."

"Not a problem." Laurel folded her tape measure and placed it in her basket. "I'm thankful for the work. I hear you're good with embroidery, something I never had the patience for, can I call on your services if I have a request for something fancy?"

"Absolutely." She added the blue flowered fabric which had been her second choice to the table for purchase.

Mildred Lowery stepped up, measured, and cut the cotton material. "Good choice of colors, Sarah."

"Thank you." She searched her bag for the bills and coins she needed for the transaction. She passed the money to Widow Lowery who wrapped the goods in white paper.

Laurel held Jesse and juggled the parcels in her other hand.

Sarah took the packages from the seamstress. "Let me help you with the bundles." She followed Laurel to her buggy and placed the goods behind the seat. Laurel passed Jesse to her and climbed in. The child put his hand on her cheeks and squeezed her face. She pushed her lips out and giggled while he laughed and put his forehead on her shoulder. She kissed his cheek and placed him beside his mother. "See you later and thank you." She waved at the little boy as his mother guided the carriage into the street.

Sarah entered the dress shop and made her way to the back where Leona worked. The wash woman pulled clothes out of a large pot. She walked into the yard and addressed the girl. "I need to go to the mercantile, do you have time to walk with me?"

Leona wrung out a man's shirt and hung it on the wire. "Got two more to go."

She sat in a chair and waited as the girl worked over the hot pot. "Laurel's making me two new dresses. I need a pair of shoes."

"Laurel's a sweet lady, she gave me a fancy dress when she married Caleb. I don't have any place to wear something so nice, but I kept it just in case. Done with this for now. Let's go."

They walked up Sidewinder Lane toward Wylder Street. Sarah's feet ached and her only concern was a new pair of shoes. With Leona beside her she didn't scan the street for Jasper and Silus so when a man grabbed her skirt she stepped back with a start and wrenched herself free.

A dirty miner stood and grabbed her arm. "Ain't you somethin'? How come I never seen you before?

His breath reeked of whiskey and her lunch rose to her throat. Suddenly Leona grabbed her away from the old man and faced the codger down. Sarah settled her hat on her head and backed away.

The feisty wash woman rose on tiptoe to bring her face even with the sooty man. "She ain't no concern of yours. Leave us be."

"Or what?"

Leona put her hands on her hip and leaned toward him. "I'll show you 'or what' you drunk piece of mule shit."

"Come on." She jerked her friend away from the man and they continued up the street. "That was brave of you."

"I learnt, you gotta give them what they deserve. Look 'em in the eye and they usually back down."

She remembered Daniel's advice, scream and run. She liked Leona's approach better. At that moment, she decided if she had to stay in this town, she would be brave like her friend. In Wylder there were drunks, gunshots during the night, rowdy miners, loose women, and gamblers. But there were good people. Jake, the shop owners, Widow Lowery, and even Miss Adelaide Willowby. Miss Willowby was her favorite of all she'd met so far. Ironic the madam of the whorehouse would become her friend. And these drunk men, down on their luck, were most likely good people at one time.

They entered the mercantile and she went straight to the area for women's boots.

Finn Wylder stopped placing men's overalls on a shelf and approached her. "Afternoon ladies, what may I assist you with today?"

She smiled at the man whom she'd served many a breakfast at Jake's Place. "Good afternoon, Mr. Wylder. I need some comfortable shoes."

Finn took a chair from behind the counter. "Have a seat, little lady and let me get you measured."

Sarah sat and tugged her boots off. "These boots are not good for standing all day. By the time the lunch crowd comes in my feet are hurting like a toothache."

Finn sized up her feet and walked behind the counter, returning with several boxes of shoes. "I think you need a lower heel with more support. Your leather shoes are nice and fancy." He picked up a boot and studied the stitching. "Good workmanship."

"They're the latest fashion, I brought them with me from Savannah, Georgia." She waited while he took the lid off several boxes.

"Try this one." He assisted her in lacing up the low-heeled boots. "Walk around a bit, see how they feel."

She walked toward Leona, who leaned against the counter. "What do you think?":

Leona squatted on the floor and squeezed Sarah's feet and checked the toes of each boot. She stood. "That's how Pa used to check my shoes and yours feel like mine do." Leona stuck her foot out. "See, my feet never hurt, I got myself some comfortable shoes from Finn last year. Ain't that right Mr. Wylder?"

Finn grinned. "You sure did, Miss Leona. I remember the day you came in and bought 'em."

Sarah sat in the chair. "I'll take them." She lifted both feet and stared. "I want to wear these now, if that's possible."

"Sure is." Finn put her old boots in the box and gave them to her. "The boots should get you through the breakfast and lunch crowd for sure."

Sarah followed the man to the front of the store and counted out the money from her purse. "They feel like gloves on my feet. Thank you for your help."

"That's what we're here for." He put the money in the drawer. "You ladies have a good day and thanks for the business."

Sarah exited the store with Leona beside her. She raised her head high and squared her shoulders. She wouldn't look down or keep her face hidden under a hat as she had in the past. She wouldn't play the victim anymore; even if the Nelsons approached, she'd stare them straight in the eye. She wouldn't seek them out but their days of bullying her were over. Her new revelation and boost of courage called for celebration. "Cross over Wylder Street. I'm buying us a treat from the bakery."

Sarah and Leona waited for a wagon to pass and hurried across the street. By the time they were in front of Doc Sullivan's office she could smell the baked goods coming from two doors down. She opened the door to the bakery and let Leona enter first. The smell of cooked butter, eggs, and flour permeated the walls. Sarah inhaled the scent and memories of the sweet shop in Savannah invoked the memory of Saturday afternoons with her mother. She stifled her emotions and searched the case. "Two of the small vanilla cakes, please." She paid with two coins and passed one to her friend. They sat on the bench in front of the store.

"Thank you." Leona ate a bite, smacking her lips. "Mighty good."

Sarah savored her cake, taking small bites and chewing slowly. Her friend ate as if she were a starving dog. She imagined Leona didn't have the money to buy treats and the idea of doing something nice for her friend filled her with warmth. People bustled around as if they had somewhere else to be. This place was so different from Georgia. She missed her daily walks to the river and the sight of the ships as they slipped through the water. She'd taken her easy life for granted.

Wylder offered nothing but dust and hard work. Though there was something in Wyoming she'd never find in Savannah: Daniel Taylor. He'd been on her mind during her waking hours and in her dreams at night. James stole her virginity, but Daniel would always be her first. The first man to take the innocence of an ignorant girl and show what a woman can feel with a man who really cared. Daniel turned the key and opened the treasure of what her body held, and she'd never forget the lesson.

Chapter Fourteen

Daniel raced the steps to Sarah's room two at a time. Saturdays were becoming Sarah's day. He'd worked extra hard during the week to finish paperwork and got up early to take care of the horses. He knocked and glanced around the street.

She gazed out the window and a beaming smile filled her face. She opened the door wide. "Good morning. You're early today."

He stepped inside and turned the lock. Sarah stood before him in a new starched yellow flowered frock. "Pretty dress."

She twirled around and then pulled her dress up to show her feet. "Got new boots, too. Laurel Holt made me two dresses. With the money I made, I was able to buy all this."

"Well, aren't you the entrepreneur." He pulled her in his arms and kissed her. Only days since he'd seen her, but every minute away from her equaled a year in his mind. She parted her lips and he growled. "I need you."

She circled her arms around his neck and melted into his embrace. "I need you." She pulled him toward the bed.

He'd planned to wait until they were at the ranch, but what the hell. She hadn't pinned her hair up and the tresses cascaded down her back. He tangled his fingers in the softness of the locks and licked her neck. Her lilac scent drove him like a wild horse. He caressed her breast, her nipple hardened at the touch of his thumb. He'd never wanted a woman this bad. She was the other part of himself. She completed the puzzle. She was the half that made him a whole person. "Sarah." He whispered her name. "My beautiful Sarah." Her blue eyes met his. They were a sapphire pool of water drawing him to the depth of her. He pulled his shirt off and started on the buttons of her dress. "I'm going to make love to you, sweetheart."

"I want you to." She stood still and let him undress her.

He would take his time to know her by heart and instill every inch of her to memory. He stripped the remainder of his clothes and laid her on the bed. He started at her toes even checking between each one. Her tiny feet had a perfect arch. He massaged both feet knowing how tired they must be from her work.

Sarah let out a breath. "That feels so good." She closed her eyes and relaxed against the pillow.

He rubbed both feet with care being careful to not tickle or cause any pain. A tiny mole on her calf drew his attention, he examined it with the tip of his finger. When he made it to her thighs, she spread her legs. The soft mound caused his hard erection to ache. Not able to wait a minute longer, he pulled apart the folds and kissed her. She gripped the sheet and lifted her hips to get closer. He teased her with licks and kisses before traveling over her belly to the plump breasts. He sucked each nipple. Her desire evident with her soft sigh.

She pulled his head to hers and kissed his mouth. "Daniel." She murmured between kisses.

He positioned himself on top of her and eased his maleness into her tight depth. They joined as one entity. He studied her face as they both approached the zenith of the crest and then collapsed in ecstasy. He rolled them to their side and they clung together on the tiny bed. "I will never have enough of you."

"Nor I, you." She whispered and raked her fingers over his back.

Goosebumps grew on his skin as her nails skimmed over him. He held her close. She was a small woman, and his hand covered the span of her back around her waist. "Sweetheart, I love you." He spoke so softly, he wondered if she perceived the words. She didn't answer him, but her mouth found his and she kissed him with timid tenderness. That was his undoing. He growled and deepened the kiss wanting to devour all of her. His erection started to come to life again. "Let's get dressed and go to the ranch." He wanted her in his bed, not in this small cot. "Lady Blue needs riding." He stood and pulled her off the bed.

"How is she? I thought about her all week." She tugged the lace chemise over her head and reached for her pantaloons.

He buttoned his trousers and pulled on his shirt. "She's adjusted to the ranch, fine. Needs riding, though." Daniel rested in the chair and pulled the leather cord from his pocket to tie his hair back.

"Leave it down." Sarah took the comb from the table and ran it through his hair.

He closed his eyes and enjoyed the moment. The only person who had groomed him was his mother and the barber back East. Since he arrived in Wyoming, he'd taken care of his beard and haircuts himself. "My turn, sit." She plopped down in the chair and he stood behind her. Before taking the comb to her tresses, he ran his fingers through the soft curls. The desire to wed this woman and share this intimacy every day brought a sense of calm to the turbulent fear of her leaving him. He placed her hat on her head. "Let's go."

Daniel secured the lock and gave Sarah the key. As she placed it in her bag, he scanned the town from the top of the stairs. The streets were crowded with wagons and people buying supplies. He escorted his woman to his buggy and assisted her into her seat. As they made their way through Wylder Street, he spotted the two men he'd been searching for. Silus sat on a bench whitling a piece of wood with a knife. Jasper glared as they passed and rested his hand on his sidearm. He nudged his brother and the man stood. He glanced at Sarah; she hadn't seen them. He slapped the reins and urged the quarter horse to a faster trot. "How was your week?"

"Jake taught me how to make biscuits." She placed her hand on her hat to keep it from coming off as the wind whipped over them. "The first biscuits I ever made were so hard I had to throw them out."

He looked her way and slowed the horse. They were well away from the Nelsons, no need to be in a hurry.

"Jake said they were easy if you did everything correctly. Said he'd not turn me loose on them by myself. If I didn't get them exactly right his customers would eat someplace else." She scooted closer.

"People are very particular about their bread." Her hand rested on his thigh. He'd never been with a woman so bold, but she did it with such innocence his chest swelled with pride to have someone like her in his life.

"How was your week?" She searched through her bag for a piece of peppermint and offered him one.

His leg ached from the absence of her touch, but he accepted the hard candy. "We went to a sale in Cheyenne. I bought a mare and Callum purchased a draft horse."

"What's a draft horse?" She searched through her drawstring bag and pulled out her essence bottle and opened the top.

He laughed as she inhaled the oil. "Sorry. Smell of the flatulence is worse when you're behind the horse." Her face reddened and he continued. "Callum purchased a Clydesdale, they originated from Scotland. Callum's wanted one since he arrived in the states. They're huge, strong work animals but are gentle enough to ride. He wants to raise them to sell. Icefall is a stallion. As soon as we find the right mare, we can breed them."

He drove the buggy under the arch on the ranch. Callum met them at the barn and Daniel threw him the reins. He stepped out of the buggy, picked Sarah up and sat her on the ground. "Ready to ride?"

"First I want to see the Clydesdale." She smoothed the wrinkles in her dress and gave the Scotsman a smile.

The trainer unleashed the horse from the carriage and rambled to a stall. "He's in the corral, follow me."

Daniel filled a bucket with water while Callum placed hay in the trough for the tired horse. The couple walked arm in arm and followed the trainer toward the fence. Icefall recognized Callum and sidled toward

Jane Lewis

them. "There he is." Daniel gestured toward the Clydesdale. "What do you think?"

She halted and placed a hand on her chest. "That is the biggest animal I've ever seen. How in the world do you get on it?"

"A large horse for a large man," Daniel chuckled. "Callum finally found one big enough for him." He took her hand and pulled her toward the corral. "He's gentle, come say hello."

Fear of the huge animal kept her knees locked in place. The horse stuck his large face over the rail, and she trailed behind Daniel. He took her hand and smoothed it over the horse's neck. "He is sweet." She moved closer and stared at his body. "His legs and feet are unusual with the long hair."

"Yes, they are quite beautiful." He rubbed the neck of the giant. "We attended a show last year in Cheyenne. An entrant from Canada brought six Clydesdales pulling a hitch. They were a sight to see, the feathering on their legs flowed as they trotted around the arena." He put his arm around her shoulder. "Callum has our horses ready. Let's ride to the creek and have a picnic. I fried chicken this morning and made biscuits."

"Sounds wonderful." She nuzzled her forehead against Icefall's face. "See you later, boy."

He held her hand as they sashayed to the barn. "Ready?" After a nod from her, he helped her mount Lady Blue.

Callum held her bridle while Daniel got on Kentucky. "Have a nice ride."

He pulled back on his reins to steady his quarter horse. "Thanks." He nodded his head toward his friend.

The Scotsman passed the straps to Sarah.

Sarah sat straight in her saddle and rode like she was born to it, but he kept Kentucky at a slow pace through the field.

Sarah eased her horse beside him. "Race you to the tree line."

"You're on." He urged Kentucky to a fast trot, Lady Blue passed them. Sarah leaned into the wind, her hair flying behind and her straw head covering straining the tie around her neck. A prettier sight he'd never seen. His girl who was afraid to get on a horse now commanding the animal as if she'd ridden all her life. He let Kentucky catch up but stayed back letting her win the race.

She pulled on the reins as Daniel approached. "We won."

"Yes, you did." He dismounted, let go of the reins so the horse could graze, and assisted her off the horse. He caught her in his arms and gave her a quick kiss before releasing her to the ground. "Hope you're hungry." Sarah took the quilt, and he carried the saddlebag and canteen to a stand of trees beside the creek.

She cleared the area of rocks before she arranged the blanket on the ground. "Your ranch is the prettiest place on earth."

Daniel took two portions of food wrapped in cloth out of the saddlebag. "Lunch is served." He passed her a fried chicken leg and biscuit. "Tell me about your home in Savannah. Do you live in town?"

"Yes, we live in the city. It's a large town with lots of people, restaurants, stores, and manufacturing facilities. You know it's right on the river. I've always loved the water; guess that's why I love this area of your ranch. We walk most places and my father and mother have a carriage if we want to venture beyond Savannah. It's a bustling city and civilized. I'm still not adjusted to the sounds of gunfire during the night in Wylder." She nibbled on her chicken.

"A change for you, as it was for me. Towns back east are years ahead of the west." He passed the canteen.

"Do you miss your home?" She drank a sip of water.

"I did for a long time." He still did until he met her. Now he wanted this to be their home. Raise their children here. Grow old together here.

They finished their lunch and he tugged her into his lap. He spread his legs and sat her in front of him, her back to his chest. Her head rested under his chin and he inhaled her flowery scent. His hands rested on her belly and she placed both of her hands on his. He could spend the rest of his life just like this and if he had his way he would. Sarah turned her head toward him and he captured her lips. After the kiss he said. "Come on, I'll show you the creek."

They walked toward the bank, the horses followed them and took a drink. Daniel sat on a large rock and removed his shoes. He stood and took her hand. "Sit down. I'll take your shoes off so we can walk in the water."

She sat on a rock and Daniel unlaced her footwear. He helped her off the rock and tied her dress around her waist. "I've waded in the ocean many times but never a creek."

He stepped in the water; it was freezing but they

would adjust. He extended his arm. "Take my hand, the rocks are slippery."

She put her toe in the water and pulled her foot back. "The water is cold as ice."

He took her hands and she stepped in the water with both feet. "This fresh water isn't warm like the Atlantic." He held her hand tight and showed her where to step.

They stood at the edge and let the water run over their feet and lower legs. Fish swam through the clear water. "Those rainbow trout make for good eating. Next time I'll bring fishing poles." He filled his hands with water and sprinkled her.

She laughed and did the same. "You're going to regret this."

He pulled her to him, their wet clothes clung to their skin. After a long kiss he carried her from the creek to the quilt. He wanted her, on his land under his tree beside his creek. She slipped out of his arms and sat on the ground. "I want you, Sarah." He fell to his knees beside her.

"I want you." She stood and removed her bloomers.

Her brazen move fired his desire like dry kindling. He removed his trousers and underpants, his heart raced in desperation. They tumbled to the quilt and he kissed her mouth with raw urgency.

She returned the passionate kiss and pulled him toward her. "Daniel," she uttered with insistence.

Desperate to love her, he swept his fingers over her most guarded place. Evidence of her want of him met his touch. He entered her soft secret center. They began the now familiar rhythm. The give and take until they were spent.

They rested in each other's arms. He acknowledged that with the turmoil in town she only felt protected with him. Truth be known he felt the same way. She made him feel safe, an experience he didn't even know existed. He pushed her hair from her face. "God, Sarah, I can't get enough of you." She rested in his embrace while he stroked her hair letting the soft curls dance through his fingers. He lifted her to a sitting position. "Better get our clothes on."

They tugged on their clothes and sat side by side on the ground. "Wyoming is the most beautiful place I've ever been." He put his arm around her. "And you're the most beautiful woman I've ever seen."

Sarah rested her head on his chest. Daniel closed his eyes and kissed the top of her head while saying a prayer of thanks to God for sending him this woman to love.

Chapter Fifteen

Sarah sat with Laurel Holt and Jesse in the parlor of the dressmaker's home. Laurel married Caleb after she arrived in Wylder with her young son. Jesse's father had abandoned them for the promise of gold. He was a typical miner searching for the next big find. She'd arrived in town with nothing but a sewing machine and a child, no money, no prospects. Widow Lowery hired her as a seamstress before she met Caleb. "Are you happy in Wylder?"

The hostess poured tea from a porcelain pot. "Compared to where Jesse and I lived, this is paradise."

"This is quite a change for me. Totally different from my home back east." Sarah took the cup and saucer and sipped the hot liquid.

Laurel removed the top from the sugar bowl. "You're from Georgia?"

"Yes, Savannah. My parents have a house in town. There are no gunshots at night or drunk men, and no cattle parading through the street." She placed a spoon of sugar in the hot tea and stirred.

"Sounds very civilized." Jesse ran to his mother and gulped down water from a glass.

Sarah laughed. "Yes, compared to Wylder, definitely civilized."

"So you decided to get on a train by yourself and venture to the west. Why?" The hostess sat and lifted the teacup to her mouth.

She didn't want to go into the details, especially with the little boy listening. "I wanted an adventure. I'd never met my mother's sister, so I decided I'd come for a visit."

Laurel handed her son a cookie and wiped his mouth with a cloth. "I see. Caleb and Daniel have been friends for several years. My husband said he's never seen him as smitten with a woman before. Daniel is our friend, and we worry he will be greatly hurt if you return to Georgia."

Sarah placed her cup in the saucer and set it on the table. "What am I supposed to do? I'll miss him, but I have my home and my parents expecting me back." Disappointing this kind man was the last thing she wanted to do, but living the rest of her life in isolation didn't appeal to her either.

Laurel tugged the child onto her lap and gave him a wooden horse. "I just know this, love finds us. Usually at the most inopportune time and there are always obstacles. You must decide if the love is worth the trouble. Giving yourself to another requires sacrifice."

Sarah swallowed the words of guilt that begged to be said. She fled to Wyoming to escape the shame she shared with her parents from her failed engagement, but the fear of hurting Daniel tore at her heart. Would she be able to say goodbye when the time came? "I gave my heart to someone, he destroyed me. I don't know if I can trust again."

"I did the same. I loved Jesse's father, but he didn't love us enough. Find someone who loves you unconditionally. If he does, there will be no doubt. It's the greatest gift in the world." She hesitated. "Can I confide in you?"

"Of course. I can keep a confidence."

"I think I may be with child but it's too soon to tell Caleb. I don't want him to know until I'm sure. He loves Jesse so much. I want to give him a child of his blood."

Sarah's gut clenched. She and Daniel had been together several times. All she wanted when they were together was him inside her, loving her. The idea of being with child did not enter her brain. How naive of her. How could she return home with a baby? Her parents would never allow it. The pounding of heavy footsteps through the house and men's voices signaled an end to their teatime.

The men entered the room, and Jesse ran to Caleb, who grabbed his son and tossed him in the air. "Are you ladies ready to go to town for dinner?"

Sarah took Daniel's outstretched hand and stood beside him. "I'm ready."

Laurel placed the teapot and cups on a tray before taking Jesse from her husband. "Will you be so kind to take these to the kitchen?"

Caleb lifted the tray. "Of course."

They waited by the front door. Sarah tickled Jesse's side and he squirmed in his mother's arms. "Thank you for the lovely tea party, Laurel."

"The pleasure was mine; you are welcome anytime." She opened the door when her husband appeared in the hall.

The families climbed in their respective carriages and journeyed toward Wylder. Daniel guided Kentucky to the road. "Did you have a nice visit with Laurel?"

"Yes, she's so sweet. It's nice to have a friend I can

talk to. She said you'd been friends with Caleb for a while." She studied his profile.

"Since I came to Wylder. He helped me when I started my ranch, introduced me to the right people, that sort of thing. They're good people." He spurred the horse to a faster pace.

"I agree. Laurel has been so kind. Caleb loves the little boy like his own." She pondered on the woman's predicament. Both she and Laurel had come to town to escape a man.

He slowed the buggy. "Jesse will only know Caleb, he'll not remember his real father."

"That's sad." She recognized that Laurel's first husband and James were cut from the same cloth. Both men irresponsible and dishonest human beings.

The wheel of the carriage dipped in the hole and he increased the pace of the horse. "In a way, but Jesse will know a man who loves and cares for him and someone who won't abandon him."

She turned to see the Holts were still behind them. "Yes, Laurel told me of some of her troubles."

"Everybody has them." He reached for her hand and placed it on his leg. "It's just easier to face when you have someone beside you."

Sarah smiled at his gesture and scooted closer, fully understanding the meaning of his words. "Do you want children?"

"I want a wife and I do want children, the more the better. And you?" He glanced her way.

"Yes, I suppose so." Her voice trailed off. "When the time comes." She trusted James and never gave a care in the world about anything except her little world in Savannah. He never mentioned children or their future, only false promises and lies.

The afternoon sun headed toward the horizon by the time the two buggies arrived in town. They stopped side by side in front of the Vincent House Hotel and Restaurant. Sarah wore one of her satin dresses today but a simpler hat and shoes to downplay the look. Daniel dressed in a white shirt and tie, black pants, and jacket. He wore his hair pulled back and tied with the leather cord. He was the most handsome man she'd ever seen. He helped her out of the carriage and the five of them entered the hotel.

Daniel led Sarah to the front desk. "We have reservations for dinner."

"Yes, sir." The man motioned for a waiter. "We'll seat your party in a few moments."

They joined their friends and Sarah continued her conversation with Laurel about the art of embroidery. "I'll teach you everything my mother taught me. She's an artist when it comes to needlework."

Laurel passed her son to Caleb. "Widow Lowery told me her sister was an expert. She says you are quite adept yourself."

Sarah reached for Laurel's arm. "Aunt Millie said that? She's done nothing but criticize me and complain about me doing work for the women at the Social Club."

"You know how the widow is, hard on the outside but I've seen a softer side of her. She was good to me and Jesse when we first arrived in town." She lowered her voice so no one could hear. "I think she's grateful for the fancy stitching on their dresses, she profits when they have a new dress made with the intention of getting your embellishments."

A restaurant attendant led them to the dining room. He pulled out a chair for each lady and passed out menus. The table was set with a white tablecloth and napkins. The waiter approached and gave them menus. "Our special today is lamb with mint sauce. He bowed and left them.

Daniel placed his menu on the table beside his plate. "I'll have the lamb. I know they get the meat from the sheep farm near Cheyenne."

The waiter returned to their table. Sarah looked up at the man and smiled. "I hear the lamb is good, I'll have that."

"Good choice." He took her menu and waited. Laurel, Caleb, and Daniel ordered the same. "I'll have your dinners out soon." He collected all the menus and left their table.

Caleb held Jesse in his lap. "Sarah, how do you like Lady Blue?"

"I love her. You know I never rode before." She placed the napkin in her lap.

He passed the boy to his mother. "Daniel told me. Everyone in the west needs to know how to ride."

"My parents own a carriage in Savannah, but my father always cared for the horse and drove the buggy. My life is so different there," she acknowledged.

"I imagine it is," Caleb said. "If you can get used to the isolation and the cold winters, you'll find this is paradise in its own way. I know you live close to the ocean and rivers, but in Wyoming we're surrounded by the beauty of mountains and streams. I can't imagine living any place else."

Laurel gave her husband a smile. "I can't either."

The tender interaction between husband and wife

caused a pang of jealousy in Sarah's heart. This couple found their home on a ranch in the wilderness close to a wild town where anything could happen. Would she be happy away from her family, friends, acquaintances she'd known her whole life? Daniel caressed her hand. Every time he touched her an electrical current flashed through her body. To spend her life never again experiencing the contact caused her muscles to tense. She smiled at him. His gaze bore into her very soul. No one had ever known her, and she'd never known another as she did him.

The waiter brought their dinner on china plates with real silver tableware. After Caleb said a prayer over the food, she took her knife and cut into the tender meat. She put a bite on her fork along with a taste of mint jelly. The pairing surprised her, but the flavor was superb. "I've never had lamb before, this is wonderful."

Laurel asked, "What do you eat in Savannah?"

"Savannah is hot most of the year. We eat a lighter diet, lots of seafood and vegetables."

Daniel took a sip of wine. "I haven't had seafood since I came west. We have good trout and river fish, though."

"You promised to take me fishing, I'm not letting you forget." She smiled at him, remembering their time at the creek.

He winked. "I'll take you real soon."

The waiter cleared their dinner plates and took orders for dessert. She and Laurel started a conversation about new fashions. The men talked of horse ranching and the ladies' talk drifted to sewing, cooking and Miss Adelaide Willowby. Both admired the madam and had nothing but nice things to say about her and her girls.

Jesse had been asleep in Caleb's lap through most of the evening. Sarah stared at the child, so innocent and precious. She put her hand on her flat stomach and imagined giving Daniel a child.

After dinner, dessert and digestif they stood outside beside their carriages. Sarah hugged Laurel. "I had such a wonderful time."

"It's always a pleasure to spend time with you." She climbed in her seat and her husband placed the sleeping boy in her lap.

Caleb joined in the response. "Certainly enjoyed seeing both of you."

She and Daniel stood in front of the restaurant; the buggy entered the street in the direction of the Holt ranch.

He broke the silence. "I'll walk you to your room."

She threaded her arm through his. For a moment she wished she could climb in his carriage and go home with him the way Laurel had with her husband. How would it feel to be Mrs. Daniel Taylor? Would he love her forever or would the situation turn out the same as her mother's friends? They avoided their wifely duties until their spouses headed to the arms of a mistress. She climbed the stairs ahead of him.

He leaned against the wall. "I had a nice evening."

"Yes, me too. Thank you." She kissed his cheek.

"Better get inside and lock the door." He waited for her to enter and close the door.

She stepped inside her small room, secured the lock, and pulled the curtain back to watch him walk up the street.

Chapter Sixteen

Saturdays drew folks to Cheyenne from all the small towns around the big city. Daniel held Sarah's hand and guided her through the crowd of people in Cheyenne. He stood back to let her enter ahead of him as they reached the Dry Goods Emporium. He guided her to the women's section and showed her a cape. Navy blue and made from thick wool, she'd need this for the cold winter days ahead. "Let me put the shawl around your shoulders."

She stood before him and wrapped herself in the fabric. "I love this." She glanced at the price. "I'll have to do more embroidery to afford it."

"I'm buying this for you. The cape caught my eye the last time Callum and I came to Cheyenne. Just wanted to make sure you approved." The deep blue accented her eyes, as he knew the color would.

"I can't let you, it's too much." She removed the heavy cape from her shoulders

"Don't argue." He folded the garment and held it in his hands. "I want you to have some plain bloomers and apparel to wear under your dresses. The lace underwear you have is pretty, but not practical." He got the attention of the store clerk.

She approached them. "May I help you, sir?"

"Yes." He gave her the cape. "We're buying this. Can you assist Sarah with some unmentionables? I'll wait for you."

"Of course." She guided Sarah toward the back.

While she shopped, he found a pair of denim pants. The ones he'd brought from Kentucky were wearing thin.

Sarah approached him with the lady in tow. "I found some plain underthings."

He smiled at the woman and followed her to the front. "I'll take these pants, also." The lady totaled their order and they waited while the items were wrapped in brown paper and tied with a rope.

Sarah took his hand. "Thank you for buying me these clothes. They're lovely. This reminds me of my favorite store in Savannah."

He gazed down at his woman. "You're welcome, sweetheart. How about lunch at the tearoom?"

"They have a tearoom?" She asked with excitement.

He'd made the right choice, he figured she'd enjoy the fancy establishment. "Cheyenne has lots of interesting places. The immigrants brought expertise from their respective countries. The shop is owned by a husband and wife from England."

They entered the small restaurant and were seated. Immediately, a teapot and cups were placed before them. Daniel poured the tea into the porcelain serving wear. He addressed the waiter. "We'll have the high tea."

"Yes sir." The man hurried away.

"You've been to this restaurant before?" Sarah placed sugar in her cup.

"Callum loves this place, believe it or not." He smiled at the memory of how much the huge man loved the delicate scones.

A plate laden with small beef turnover pies, chicken sandwiches, and fruit was placed before them. Another plate with scones, clotted cream, and small desserts was placed to her right. "This looks wonderful."

She filled a scone with cream before taking a bite. "I wish I had the recipe for these."

He placed a turnover on his plate. "Callum says it's just a sweet biscuit. You use butter instead of lard and cream instead of milk and add a little sugar. He made them for me with raisins. If you know how to make Jake's biscuits, you can make the scones." He tore the pie open to reveal chopped beef and gravy.

"I'm going to give them a try. Wonder if the cowboys would eat them for breakfast?" She laughed.

He returned her smile. "The men in Wylder eating scones, I'd love to see that."

They finished their meal and Daniel led her from the tearoom to the photography studio. He wanted a picture to remember her in case she left on the next train home. "Let's get a photograph."

She entered the establishment and inspected the photography on display while he spoke to the proprietor.

"Come, Sarah. I want a picture of you." He led her to the back.

She sat in a chair while the man prepared his equipment.

The photographer turned her shoulders slightly to her right side and had her turn her head toward him. He took the photo and went to a back room with his equipment. He returned a short time later and showed them the picture.

Daniel scrutinized the art. "Beautiful. I want one of us together."

The photographer seated Daniel in the chair. "Now, you stand beside him."

Sarah stood beside the chair.

The man placed her hand on Daniel's shoulder. "Be as still as possible." He took the picture. "Let me develop this one."

"Will you let him take one of you by yourself?" She asked. "I want one for my room, so I don't feel so alone. I'll pay."

Daniel pulled her to him. "Of course, sweetheart. And no need for you to pay."

The man returned with the tin type. "What more can I help you with?"

Daniel replied. "The lady wants a picture of me."

He sat Daniel in a chair. "Look straight at me."

She hurried to the chair. "Wait." She pulled the leather cord from his hair and let his tresses fall around his face.

Daniel smiled. Why didn't he think to take off her hat and let her hair fall at her shoulders? The man took the picture and returned a few minutes later. He paid him and they exited the store with their packages and photographs.

He assisted her into the carriage, and they left town headed west to Wylder. He yearned to take her to the ranch, but the hour grew late, and he wanted her settled in her room before the riffraff started in town.

They were just outside Cheyenne when Kentucky sped his pace from a trot to a gallop. Daniel struggled to keep the animal from bolting. Thundering horse hooves approached from behind. Daniel glanced around while struggling to keep the carriage from overturning. Two men on horseback with bandanas over their face raced toward them. The horses passed them and stopped in the middle of the road. He pulled the carriage to a halt, and Kentucky reared. He settled the animal and held the reins tight.

Sarah grabbed his arm. "What's happening?"

The men on horseback were beside the buggy before he could draw his gun. "Be calm," he whispered. "I'll handle this." He instinctively placed a hand on his sidearm.

"I wouldn't do that if I were you," the man on the right said. "All we want is your money but if you give us any trouble, we'll take the lady, too."

Daniel had placed their parcels under their seat and hoped they wouldn't search the carriage. He gave her the leads. "Hold tight." He removed his money clip from his pocket. "It's all I've got." He handed over his money.

The bandit threw the clip to his accomplice and counted the money. "It'll do."

The horses pranced beside the carriage. The men held the reins tight as if they weren't ready to leave. Daniel's blood ran cold in his veins. The man on his left raked his eyes over Sarah. His legs tensed and he started to rise from his seat when the man with the stolen money nodded his head toward Cheyenne and they left in the same direction they came.

Daniel held Sarah's hands in his. She shook with fright and he wanted to calm her, but he had to scurry before the men changed their mind and came back for her. "I'm sorry and I know you're scared but I've got to get us back quick before they or someone else decides to attack or follow us."

"Let's go." She placed her hand on his leg and held onto his thigh.

He urged Kentucky to as fast a gallop as possible without risking turning the buggy over. If Sarah hadn't been with him, he'd have put up a fight. What if they had taken her? He didn't recognize the men. He was sure they'd seen them together in Cheyenne which made them easy targets. Kentucky kept the pace. He wanted to escape to the ranch as much as Daniel. As they approached his land, he slowed the carriage, the horse trotted to the barn without instruction.

"You're stopping at the ranch before we go to town?"

He breathed a sigh of relief as they went under the arch toward his house. "Not taking you back. You're staying with me tonight. Your aunt can spread as many rumors as she wants. I don't care."

She squeezed his arm. "I don't either."

Callum came from the barn. "Never seen Kentucky kick up as much dirt. What's got into him? See a snake?"

Daniel pulled the leads and drew the buggy to a halt. "We were robbed on the way back. Just outside Cheyenne. Two riders. Didn't see their faces because of the bandanas, didn't recognize the horses, either."

"What'd ye give 'em?" He calmed Kentucky while Daniel helped Sarah from the carriage.

"Got the remainder of the money I had, and the gold money clip my father gave me. About fifty dollars." He steadied Sarah. He gazed into her eyes to read if she was okay.

"I'll get me rifle and we'll track the bastards down." He said as he unharnessed the horse from the carriage.

"No." He collected the parcels from the buggy.

Callum held Kentucky by his reins. "How no?"

"Because they're long gone by now and I don't want to bring any more attention to us." He nodded his head toward his girl.

"Aye. I'll take care of Kentucky and the buggy. Ye both tuck in for the night." The Scotsman winked.

They approached the stairs to his house. "Wait, let me put the packages beside the door." He stalked up the stairs and placed them on a table then turned and hurried back for Sarah. He led her up the steps. After he unlocked the front door, he guided her to a settee in the library. "I'll be right back." He hurried to the door and retrieved their packages. They weren't followed but the unease wouldn't dissipate.

He splashed a finger of whiskey in a glass for him and poured her a sherry. "This will make you feel better." He handed her the small glass. He stood by the fireplace with his elbow on the mantel and studied her. His first instinct was to take her in his arms and hold her, forever if he had to.

Sarah sipped her sherry until the glass was empty, then stepped to the liquor table. "I'll take a little more."

He filled her glass and placed the carafe on the table. "Are you okay?" He passed the glass to her.

She drank a sip and walked to the window. "We're lucky they didn't kill us, aren't we?" She pulled the curtain back and stared into the yard.

Or worse, take you away from me. "Yes, lucky. These men just wanted money. I don't believe they were bad men like Jasper and Silus Nelson, most likely needed money for their families. There's lots of people down on their luck. It only takes one bad crop year, or a mining bust to turn a good man bad." He poured another drink in his glass and drank it in one gulp. He turned and she stood beside him.

"Daniel, hold me." She put her glass on the table and reached her arms around his neck.

Her quiet sobs broke his heart. "I've got you." Please don't make me let you go, he prayed from his soul. "You're safe. I won't let anything happen to you." He gathered her in his arms and transported her upstairs. "I want you to rest and forget about what happened today."

She slid from his embrace, her feet touched the floor and she stood before him. "I didn't know there could be so much danger and bad people in this world."

He turned down the bed clothes. "The west is a mixing pot of individuals. Most of them are good, honest, hardworking but some are greedy for gold and anything they can steal from others."

She wiped her face dry of the spent tears and walked to the other side of the bed and helped. "I don't cry easily. Seems all the things I've been through since I left home crashed down on me. Makes me realize what a sheltered life I've led."

He retrieved a sleep shirt from his bureau and removed her clothes. "This will be more comfortable." He helped her into the oversized shirt, folded her clothes neatly, and placed them in a chair. "Lay down and rest. I've a few things to do and then I'll be right up." He tucked her in and kissed her forehead.

Daniel poured another drink and sipped. He

unwrapped the photos, stared at the tintype of Sarah and placed the frame on his desk so he could see it every day. The Kentucky mash relaxed his mind and he pondered over the danger Sarah faced alone in Wylder. A Colt Deringer rested in the drawer of his desk. Daniel pulled the gun out and checked the box of bullets. This would be perfect for Sarah.

He lit a candle and extinguished the oil lamp. He'd climbed the stairs holding this candle holder in his hand many nights but never to her waiting in his bed. Her soft snore greeted him as he entered the room. He sat the light on the dresser and positioned the tintype of them in a predominate place so the picture would be the first thing he set his eyes on each morning when he woke. The woman asleep in his bed caused his groin to ache and his arousal strained against his pants. He sat in a chair and removed his clothes, climbed in the bed without disturbing her and enveloped her in his arms. She snuggled against him. Sleep evaded him as the day's events played in his mind. He'd read the eyes of the men who robbed them. The leader only wanted money as he'd said but the other man's eyes radiated evil and the way his gaze raked over Sarah still gave him chills. The facts were true, he could have done nothing to prevent what happened.

Sarah woke and climbed on top of him. She kissed his cheek, his forehead, and the tip of his nose before her lips settled on his mouth.

He deepened the kiss and she moaned. His desire was to brand her, make everyone know she belonged to him. She tugged the shirt over her head and threw it on the floor. Her silky, pale skin exposed itself to him from the light of the moon. He sucked on her nipple as she leaned into him and settled herself on top. He devoured her lips and entered her. She found her rhythm, his hips kept time with hers as they climbed higher and higher to the peak. Her tender cry when she came and the tightness as she convulsed around him caused him to spill his seed inside her. He groaned and called her name. He positioned her beside him, and they spooned together, her body protected by his.

A tear of happiness slid down his face. He found the desire of his heart with Sarah.

Chapter Seventeen

Sarah woke to a heaviness around her body. Daniel had his arm around her and his leg over her legs. She smiled and settled into the embrace remembering the love they'd given each other. She wiggled and his erection came to life.

He kissed her neck and turned her toward him. "I want you." He found her lips and rolled her to her back.

He claimed her with his passionate kiss, and she surrendered. Her center demanded the joining. Last night, the darkness kept her shyness at bay, and she'd taken control, listened to her greedy body, and made love to him. The intense feeling of being on top and the heat that rushed through her body when she landed on the crest lasted longer than it ever had. Daniel had control now and he pounded into her. The bed squeaked as it moved across the slick wooden floor. She closed her eyes and rode with him. The mounting surge overtook her, she cried out. He kissed her, his tongue explored as he poured himself into her and groaned.

He pulled her close and held her tight against him. "How do you feel this morning, my love?"

"Safe." She whispered.

He smoothed her hair. "I won't let anything happen to you."

His muscular body enveloped hers. "I know." They rested in the quiet house. There was no shouting or men chasing women, no gun shots. All was quiet.

The curtains danced from a soft breeze, and the sun beamed in the bedroom window. Sarah snuggled closer to Daniel and closed her eyes. She didn't want to think about going back to Wylder. Daniel rose from the bed where a chill from the light wind teased her back.

He tucked the blankets around her. "I'm going to get a bath ready for you downstairs. You rest a while longer and I'll call you when it's ready." He sat on the bed and dressed.

She sat up. "I should help."

He rested his hands on her shoulders and placed her back in bed. "No, I want you to rest."

She fell into the pillows and pulled the sheet around her. "If you insist. I'm still a little tired."

He finished dressing and placed the sleep shirt on the back of the chair. "Wear my shirt when you come downstairs. I'm taking your clothes with me. I'll freshen them."

Wide awake, she gazed around his bedroom. The brightness of the morning sun reflected in the mirror over the chest. A rooster crowed and the birds sang their morning songs. His footsteps echoed through the house. She stretched and her eyes caught sight of the tintype of them together. He must have placed it on the dresser while she slept. She slid out of bed and tiptoed across the cool wood floor. She picked up the picture and stared at his handsome face. Another picture caught her eye. This one had to be his parents because the man looked like an older version of Daniel and just as handsome with his gray hair and beard. The woman was beautiful for an older lady. Hope of being Daniel's wife swelled her heart until she remembered if she married him, she would never go home. She'd have to live in this lawless town the rest of her life. Her body chilled from the morning air. She crossed the floor and donned the sleep shirt, walked to the window, and gazed into the yard. She turned at the sound of footsteps in the hallway. Daniel leaned against the door frame. His handsome face held a smile as he raked his eyes over her body.

He approached her and smoothed her hair. "Bath is ready."

She crossed the floor and picked up the framed picture. "Your parents?"

"Yes. They sent the picture to me last Christmas." He stared at the photograph. "I haven't seen them since I arrived, five years ago. They said they might visit next spring."

"I can't imagine going one year without seeing my parents." Though her homesickness had eased up since she'd met friends and Daniel.

He escorted her downstairs and helped her in the tub. "Take your time, I need to do some work."

"This is heaven." She slid as low in the tub as she could, letting the warm water tease her neck.

He retrieved a bar of soap from the kitchen. "Sorry, this is all I have. I know you like the floral scents, but this will have to do."

"I love the smell of this, reminds me of you." She wet the rag and lathered it with soap. "Do you have ingredients for biscuits? I want to make them for breakfast."

"How about if I get some cream and butter from Callum? There's flour and sugar in the pantry. You can make scones."

She rested in the tub with the water up to her neck. "Sounds wonderful. You said to use the recipe for biscuits, and use a little sugar to sweeten them, and butter instead of lard, and cream instead of milk?"

"That's how Callum makes them." He turned to leave. "Your clothes are on the chair."

She smiled and closed her eyes, letting the warmth of the water relax her. "Thank you." She hoped the water would wash away the terror from the day before.

Sarah held her breath and put her head under water. When she rose, water splashed on the floor. She waited until the small waves settled and washed her hair with Daniel's soap. She wanted the smell of him on her entire body. When the water grew cold, she got out and dried herself with the large flour sack. She dressed and let her damp hair fall around her shoulders and mopped the spilled water from the floor with the drying cloth.

Sarah entered the kitchen and examined the space. The room had a wall of shelves on one side filled with blue and white china dishes. On the lower shelves were everyday pewter plates and cups. This was a modern kitchen by the west's standards. Using the water pump in the sink, she filled a cup of water for drinking and a coffee pot to the brim. Daniel had the wood stove hot and ready for baking. She placed coffee in the basket and settled the pot on the stove. Jake would love this large kitchen, he prepared food for the restaurant in one half this size.

Daniel entered with a crock of butter and a pail of cream. "Callum sent raisins." He sat the bowl of dried fruit on the table. "Said they would be good in the scones. Told him we'd save him some."

She stared at the ingredients and reminded herself

how to make biscuits. "If they're good. I've made biscuits twice and never made scones."

He pulled her in his arms. "I'm sure they'll be delicious."

"You have a lot of confidence in me." She gazed into his eyes; they were dark brown pools of glass that bored into her soul. She could lose herself in them and never find her way out.

"I think you've got all you need to get started. I've got to feed the chickens and gather eggs." He kissed her before he hurried from the room.

She placed the ingredients on the worktable. Jake's voice sounded in her head. "Don't mix the dough too long, the bread won't be flaky." She cut the scones in triangles to match the ones from the restaurant, placed them on the tray, and put them in the hot oven. The large rocking chair in the corner proved the perfect place to sit and sip coffee while the scones baked. The kitchen was bright with light and cool from the morning breeze wafting through the large windows that surrounded a rock fireplace. The smell of the bread wafted through the kitchen and she jumped from the chair, leaving it rocking without her weight, and ran to the stove. Taking up a thick rag to protect her hands from the heat she removed the pan from the oven. The scones were perfectly light brown. Daniel had placed a blue and white Wedgewood platter on the worktable, and she arranged the scones in the dish.

Daniel came in the kitchen with a basket of eggs. "Smells heavenly."

She poured him a cup of coffee and placed the platter of scones on the table. "I hope they're good." She waited as he tried the warm bread.

"Delicious." He placed another on his plate and reached for the butter.

Callum entered and walked straight to the coffee pot. "Smells just like me home in Scotland in here." He grabbed a scone and took a bite. "Tastes like it, too."

The men placed more scones on their pewter plates. Daniel winked at her.

Elated that they enjoyed her food she asked, "Do you really think they're good?"

Daniel stood and pulled out a chair for her to sit with them at the table. "Have you tasted them?"

"No." She removed one from the plate and broke it open. She ate a bite and scrutinized her work. The flaky buttery scone filled with raisins tasted better than the ones she had yesterday. "They are delicious. Beginners luck, I guess."

She listened as the men planned their day. Sundays on a ranch were no different than any other. Animals had to be fed and watered and cared for. "You can take me back to town, I don't want to hinder your work."

Daniel tilted his head and stared. "You'll never be in my way. I've got a few things to do and then I'll be free the rest of the day."

Callum finished his coffee and breakfast. "Cow needs milking." He stood and placed his dish wear in the sink. "Thanks for the delicious scones, Miss Sarah."

"I'm happy you liked them." She cleared the remainder of the dishes from the table.

Daniel placed a cloth over the platter of scones. He kissed her cheek. "I'll be back soon."

She busied herself in the house cleaning the dishes, then wiped down the surfaces and swept the floor.

Daniel came inside through the front of the house.

The echo of boots hitting the wood floor rang through the kitchen. A hunt through the house found him in his office searching through a desk drawer. He pulled out a gun and her heart did a flip in her chest. "Is something wrong?" She prayed the robbers hadn't found where he lived.

"Everything is fine. Ever shot a gun before?"

Her hand went to her throat. "No. Never." A gun and the loud sound they made scared her. She had enough of gunshots in the night to last her lifetime.

"If you insist on going back to town, I want you to have a gun. This one is small and easy to use. You can keep the pistol in your pocket, and no one will even know you have one." He put three bullets in the handgun. "This is a three shooter." He filled his pocket with bullets. "I set up a practice area away from the house."

She sat in a chair. A gun. Her father had a gun for protection but never used it. The finality of her predicament filled her. She was alone in town; anyone could take her. He was right this was her only choice. If she stayed at the dress shop until time for her to go home, she needed protection.

She followed him through the house to the kitchen door. The area was filled with farm animals. They trudged past the chicken coop where hens cackled, and a rooster crowed over his harem. The milk cow who grazed in a large fenced-off area stopped chewing and mooed as they passed. When they were good distance from the house, she smelled a strong odor and covered her nose with her hand. Pigs wallowed in a muddy pen grunting and squealing. They hurried past them and came to a large opening in the woods. Stacked hay bales stood a few yards away.

He pulled the gun from his pocket. "This is the hammer. You pull it back, aim and pull the trigger." He shot the gun.

She immediately covered her ears at the sound.

"Aim for the middle of the circle." He fired the gun twice more, hitting the target each time. He loaded the derringer and placed it in her hand. "Your turn."

Her hand shook with the weight of the gun.

"Don't be nervous. Pull the hammer back and aim at the target."

The gun felt heavy in her hands and the hammer difficult to pull. She managed to follow his instructions and pointed the gun in the direction of the hay bale. Her hand went up as the gun fired and she missed the target.

He stood behind her and steadied her arm with his hands. "Line your sight with the target."

She did as he said, and his confidence radiated in her body. "I see the bullseye."

"Pull the hammer back and pull the trigger."

The gun fired and her body repelled into his. She came closer to the middle of the target.

"Again," he said.

She followed his orders. The shot was almost as good as his.

"Good shooting." He filled the derringer with bullets. "Practice, so I'll know you've got this."

She took aim as he taught her and fired once, twice, three times. Each shot closer to the middle of the target. "Once you get used to the noise and feel, it's kind of fun."

"I'll feel better if you have this with you when you're alone. Will you keep the derringer in your pocket?" He studied her face for an answer.

She placed the gun in the pocket of her dress. "Yes, I'll keep it with me."

Chapter Eighteen

Sarah entered the dress shop with the basket containing Miss Willowby's needlework. Several women milled around the store, searching for fabric and thread to sew their own clothing. Saturday mornings were Widow Lowery's busiest day. It was the time the women rode into town with their husbands. While the men loaded up on animal feed and supplies, the women shopped at the apothecary, the mercantile, and the dress shop. She approached her aunt. "Morning, Widow Lowery."

"Sarah, everything good with you?" The old woman unpacked a box of thread.

"Yes ma'am. Here's my board money." She placed two dollars on the table.

The old woman put the coins in her pocket. "Need you and Leona to take a bag of sewing out to Laurel. Can you drive a buggy?"

She'd never commanded a carriage and the request gave her pause but the idea of an adventure with Leona seemed like a fun way to spend her day off work. "I can try."

"Leona can if you can't. Tell Chet to set you up in a small buggy and charge it to my account." She placed the canvas bag on the table.

Sarah made her way to the alley behind the store. She positioned the basket and sewing in the chair. "I need to take this basket to The Social Club and Widow Lowery wants us to take the sewing to Laurel. Said to get a buggy from Chet. Do you know how to drive a carriage?"

The wash woman poured hot water in the pot. "Everyone knows how to drive a buggy."

"Can I help do something?" She stood beside the hot pot of water.

"Just pulled these out of the tub. You hold the basket while I hang 'em on the line." She draped men's shirts along the heavy string.

"We'll go by the Social Club on our way to the livery." Sarah followed her friend with the clothes basket.

The wash woman worked swiftly through the clothesline until all was draped and blowing in the wind." Don't know if I'd be welcome in the Social Club."

"Don't be silly." She put the clothes basket on the ground and retrieved the bag and basket.

They scurried through the back street to the brothel. The stares from the drunks didn't scare her. The gun in her pocket and walking with Leona gave her courage.

They approached the Social Club and she had to drag Leona up the steps. "Don't be afraid, everyone here is nice." She rapped the door knocker and the guard greeted them. "Hi, Abraham. Is Miss Adelaide in?"

He stepped aside. "Yes'm, she's here."

"Thank you." She entered and looked behind for Leona.

The girl stood on the porch staring at Abraham.

"You're the biggest man I ever seen."

He chuckled. "Come in, I ain't gonna bite." He escorted them to the madam's office.

Miss Willowby rose from her seat behind the desk. "You've completed the cape already? My, you do work fast. And who do you have with you?" She approached Leona and tilted the wash woman's chin and studied her face. "Leona Fabray, I don't think you know what a beautiful girl you are. Why do you wear men's clothes?"

Leona stepped back. "The way I dress is my business."

"Beautiful and spunky." The madam sat and motioned for them to sit. "You might ought to keep dressing in this fashion, I don't think there's a man in this town that could handle you."

Sarah passed the basket to the madam. "I hope you approve."

Miss Adelaide peeled back the white fabric and gazed at the shawl folded within. She ran her hand over the fine embroidery. "You do beautiful work." She stood, examined the cape, and draped it over her shoulders. "This is exactly what I had envisioned." She removed the shawl and studied the needlework. "Lovely." She opened a desk drawer and passed money to Sarah. "I'll have more jobs for you, soon. Some of the girls want to fancy up their clothes, too."

She placed the money in her reticule. "I appreciate the business. I'll have the other work you gave me ready soon."

The madam stood and walked to the door in search of her assistant. "Miss McCarthy, show the ladies out, please."

The housekeeper waited in the hallway for them to exit the office and led them through the house. "You girls have a nice day."

They said their goodbyes and darted up Old Cheyenne Road toward the livery. The Nelson brothers sauntered out of the Five Star Saloon. Silus elbowed his brother and pointed. She fingered the cold metal of the gun in her pocket and her blood ran cold through her veins. Jasper walked toward them; his hand hovered over his sidearm. She picked up her pace toward the livery. "Hurry, the Nelsons spotted us." She raised the hem of her dress and ran, trying to keep up with Leona's pace. The wash woman had the advantage in her men's pants and boots. They made it to the livery and Leona took charge of the buggy while Sarah instructed Chet to charge the fee to the dress shop.

Sarah relaxed as her friend guided the carriage out of town toward the Holt Ranch. She searched the street and alleys for the Nelson brothers. Assured they were gone, she settled into the ride. Leona handled the carriage with the skill of a man. They turned into the drive and headed toward the house.

Laurel greeted them. "What do I owe this visit?"

Sarah eased out of the carriage and smoothed her dress. Her nerves still jangled from the encounter in town.

Leona jumped to the ground and tied the reins to the hitching post. "Widow sent us out here to bring some work to you."

Sarah passed the bag to the seamstress. "Here you go."

Laurel took the sewing and led them to the front door. "Must be a rush job, Widow Lowery doesn't spend money to send sewing to me unless someone pays extra. Come in and I'll fix us a cup of tea."

They followed her inside. Sarah examined the spotless house. The wood furniture smelled of lemon and the wood gleamed as if just rubbed down with beeswax. The house appeared different with the midday sun shining through the lace curtains.

Jesse sat on the floor and played with a small wooden wagon filled with blocks. "Hello, Jesse," Sarah said as she entered the room.

He glanced at her. "Hi," he said and went back to his game.

"Have a seat and I'll be back in a moment." Laurel settled them in the parlor and headed toward her kitchen.

They took their seats on the settee. Sarah gazed around the familiar room. A family lived in this house, there were children's toys, Laurel's sewing machine, and Caleb's desk topped with books and papers. If she married Daniel, would his house become their home? She imagined her personal things mixed with his. Would she find happiness in Wyoming? Laurel thrived on the ranch, but she wasn't Laurel, she was Sarah Miller from Savannah, Georgia.

Their hostess entered the room with a tray filled with tea and cookies. "I baked these yesterday. Didn't know I'd have company." She poured tea into cups and passed around the treats.

Sarah sipped from a rose appliqued cup and nibbled at a cookie. "These are delicious."

"Thank you." Laurel pulled Jesse in her lap and gave him a sip of milk from a glass. "How are you adjusting to Wylder, Sarah?"

"It's not what I'm accustomed to. I want to be back home by Christmas." Sarah's mother promised to write her when the gossip dissipated. She hoped it would be before the snow set in.

"What about Daniel? Last we were together you seemed serious about each other." Laurel passed the cookies around again.

Leona chose two of the treats. "They are serious, and they look handsome in his fancy carriage."

Sarah placed her cup and saucer on the table. "Laurel, Caleb knows Daniel well. What does he think of him?"

"Daniel Taylor is one of the most upstanding of gentlemen. Caleb has done business with him for years. They have the same values when it comes to raising animals. I've seen both men take back horses after they sold them if the buyer abused the animal. Why do you ask? Have you seen anything different?" She poured tea into Sarah's cup.

Sarah added sugar and cream to her drink and contemplated her answer. "What I told you about before, the man in Savannah fooled me and my family. He appeared to be an upstanding gentleman. He wasn't."

"Daniel is a good man." Laurel said in a calm voice.

Sarah raised the porcelain cup to her lips. "Not that Mr. Taylor would even ask me to stay in Wylder and marry him."

Laurel walked toward her son, scooped him from the floor and placed him on her hip. "Would him proposing be a bad thing?"

"No, I suppose it wouldn't." She remembered their

day in Cheyenne and how much fun they had together.

"At one time, I loved Jesse's father. He wasn't a bad man, but he put his want of gold and riches over Jesse and me. Caleb found me when I didn't want to be found and showed me and Jesse how pure love can be." She tousled her son's hair. "I wish the same for you and Leona. You both deserve a good man."

"I ain't lookin' for no man." Leona set her drink on the table. "Guess we better get back, I got clothes to wash."

Sarah stood and arranged their soiled dishes on the silver tray. "Thank you for a lovely time. I've always enjoyed afternoon tea."

Laurel stood with Jesse in her arms. "Please come back again."

They exited the house while Laurel stood in the door holding the boy. "We will," Sarah said as she strolled toward the buggy.

Leona turned the carriage toward town. "I enjoyed the visit but if we don't get back, I'll be working 'til dark."

The impromptu tea party with Laurel and Leona stirred Sarah's homesickness. She missed her friends and their daily visits. Her work at Jake's Place and the extra embroidery from Miss Adelaide kept her anxiety at bay until she was reminded of better times.

Sarah held onto her hat as Leona took the horse to a fast trot. The sound of horse hooves approaching from behind made her heart pound, and her hands grew numb from fear. She turned; her stomach took a dive. Two men on horseback approached at a fast pace. She prayed it wasn't the robbers from Cheyenne. "Leona, do you have anything of value on you?"

"No." She urged the animal to a faster pace. "You think they're robbers?"

"Could be the same ones who accosted Daniel and me." She turned. The riders thundered toward them.

"They might just be in a hurry." Leona concentrated on the road ahead. "Maybe I should slow and let them pass. They're gonna catch us anyway."

Sarah gazed back as the riders approached and recognized Jasper and Silus. She put her hand in her pocket and fingered the gun. Before she could get it out, the men were on them with their pistols drawn.

"Stop the buggy." Jasper yelled.

"Don't," Sarah pleaded. "Keep going."

Leona continued almost colliding with Silus's horse. The carriage teetered and then righted itself.

A gunshot rang out and Sarah's heart skipped a beat. "Do what they say."

Leona pulled the reins. "Whoa," she shouted.

Jasper put his gun in his holster. "I've got you now." He edged his horse close to the carriage. "Climb on. You're comin' with us."

Her tea and cookies rose in her throat. She swallowed and mustered every ounce of courage she possessed. "I'm not going anywhere with the likes of you."

Silus cocked his pistol. "Do what he says, or I'll kill you right here and leave you for the buzzards. Both of you. Your friend first, so you can watch her die."

The image of Leona dead from a bullet brought her to her feet. "No need." Jasper helped her on his saddle in front of him. His arm tightened about her waist. He had the same sour smell. Her stomach heaved and the food she ate rose from her belly. She gagged and leaned her head so the vomit would fall to the ground.

Jasper steadied his horse and balanced Sarah in front of him. "If Daniel Taylor wants to see his whore again, he needs to bring us five thousand dollars. Tell 'im to bring it to the old Powell farm."

The man's strong hold around her waist kept her from falling. Her shoulders slumped and her muscles congealed like muscadine jelly. The dizziness overtook her, she remembered nothing until they stopped. She opened her eyes, and the fear of her predicament caused a dry heave.

Jasper called to Silus. "Come and get her before she pukes on me." He handed her off to his brother.

Sarah put her hands on her knees and lost everything left in her stomach. Perspiration beaded on her face and her legs wobbled from lack of strength. She grabbed the porch rail to steady herself.

Jasper pulled a fist back and punched her in the face. "That's for the kick in the balls."

The blow knocked her off her feet and she stumbled backwards. Her body hit the hard ground and her tailbone ached as if it was on fire. Anger spilled through her as her nostrils flared and her pulse quickened; if they wanted a fight, she'd give it to them. Her hand found her pocket but before she could pull out her derringer, he yanked her in the cabin and deposited her in a chair.

"Sit down, bitch." He yelled. "Silus, look for rope."

Jasper stood beside her chair, but his attention was on the layout of the room. She took the few moments to gather her wits and plan her next move. Something wet rolled down her cheek. She touched it and examined her finger. Blood. She pulled her skirt and wiped around the cut. The skin around her eye burned and her head ached from the assault.

Jasper gazed down at her. "Do not move." He knocked a hole in the window shutter with a metal rod.

Sarah gazed around the shack and searched for a way out. She fingered the gun, but she couldn't shoot them both. She quickly removed the scissors from her pocket and hid them in the palm of her hand. The only other furniture in the room was an old table in the middle of the floor. Silus emptied debris from drawers on the bare table. Her gaze darted to the back of the cabin and the rear door that stood wide open.

The younger brother pulled a skein of thick string from the rubble. "This is all I can find."

Jasper grabbed the twine and squatted behind the chair. "Put your hands behind your back." He secured her wrists, moved to the front of her chair, and raised his hand to hit her.

She turned her head, ready for the blow. She winced as the movement caused the ties to pierce her skin.

Jasper spit on the wood floor. "Skittish, are you? I'm gonna have fun with you."

She held back a scream and wished she had the gun in her hand instead of the scissors. Killing Jasper would be worth risking her life with Silus. Air forced into her lungs in bursts. If she got out of here alive, she'd have to calm herself enough to think clearly. It was ten steps to the back door, but she estimated she could run it in six.

Silus asked his brother, "What are we going to do when he brings the money?"

"We'll kill 'im. She's ours now." The man stared

out the window.

She went to work on the cord as soon as their backs were turned. She rotated her wrists. Her skin was sore, and burned from the tightness of the rope. The small scissors weren't made to cut thick twine. Her hand cramped from the position and the fear of dropping the clippers weighed on her mind. She used the implement to cut through a loop. The twine unraveled and she caught it in her free hand right before it slipped off her wrist. She held the scissors in one hand and the rope in the other. Unless they stood behind her, they'd never know she'd freed herself. When Daniel came, she'd run outside and warn him. The men paid her no attention now, they waited for the cash.

"You think he's got that much money?" Silus asked his brother.

"He's got it all right, or he'll find it." Jasper turned to gloat.

She looked him in the eye and stared him down. Her fear had transformed into the bravery she needed to keep her and Daniel alive.

Jasper pulled his pistol from the holster and stepped outside, Silus followed close behind him. Now was her chance. She scampered like a squirrel out the back door.

Chapter Nineteen

Daniel led the quarter horse around the arena. The stallion had spirit. This was the third day of getting the animal accustomed to a bridle and him.

Callum jumped off the fence and walked toward him. "I'll have a go."

He passed the reins to the Scotsman. "You may have better luck."

The horse bucked as a carriage thundered down the path to the ranch. A woman's voice screaming his name sounded through the afternoon air. He ran from the corral with a feeling of dread rising from his gut.

"Mr. Taylor, Mr. Taylor!" Leona Fabray stopped the buggy and jumped to the ground. "Hurry, Mr. Taylor, they got Sarah." She bent at the waist and held her stomach, gasping for breath.

He and Callum ran to the carriage. Callum grabbed the reins.

Daniel's voice almost left him. "Who has Sarah?" He grabbed Leona by her shoulders and pulled her to standing.

"The Nelson brothers," the girl panted. "They're at the old Powell farm. Said for you to bring five thousand dollars or they'd kill her."

"Get to town and tell Sheriff Hanson. Tell him to meet us there." He turned to Callum. "Give her horse some water and saddle ours."

Daniel ran in the house and went straight to his safe. He counted out five thousand dollars and put it in a saddlebag. His mistrust of banks was a godsend today. He put his gun belt on and checked the bullets in his revolver. He stuffed another small pistol in his trousers behind his back. His knife with the leather sheath fit inside his boot. With all he needed for the rescue, he raced out the door.

Callum had mounted Finlay, his rifle hung in the saddle scabbard. He held the reins to Kentucky. "What's the plan?"

"The plan is we get her away from the bastards." He mounted Kentucky and placed the saddlebag in front of him.

"Whoa." Callum called. "Not so fast, I said what's the plan. Gotta have a plan or we all get killed."

Kentucky pranced, ready to go. "When we get close, we'll dismount and leave our rides far enough away the Nelsons won't know we're there. I'll walk to the front; they won't hear me coming until I'm right on them. You go to the back, close enough to hear what's going on. We've got to get Sarah out no matter what happens to me. I've got the money. If they don't deal, kill them." He spurred Kentucky to a gallop, Finlay hot on his tail.

Daniel cursed and spurred Kentucky faster. He didn't keep her safe. It was his fault, his damn fault. Wylder, Wyoming was no place for a young single woman. Especially one from a sheltered home in the East. He hoped giving her the derringer and teaching her how to shoot would keep her safe. One man maybe, but there were two after her.

They dismounted a few yards from the farm and

secured the mounts. Daniel and Callum picked their way through overgrown pines and brush to the old farmhouse. He waited until the Scotsman was in position behind the cabin. At the sound of a bird call, he made his way to the front.

The door opened, and Jasper stood with his pistol pointed at Daniel. "That the money?"

Daniel lifted the bag. "Five thousand dollars. Where's Sarah?"

"Put the bag on the ground and take off your gun belt." Jasper stepped close to the edge of the porch.

He placed the holstered gun on the ground next to the money. He put his hands up. "You've got your money, give me the girl."

Jasper kept his focus on Daniel. "Silus, get the money and his gun." He waited until his brother stepped away, and pointed his gun at Daniel's head. "You ain't gettin' the girl. She's ours now."

The telltale sound of a rifle being cocked sounded from the side of the house. Daniel pulled the gun from its hiding place. "Now you drop your guns. Sheriff's on his way."

Jasper pulled back the hammer on his gun.

A shot rang out from the other side of the house, Jasper dropped to the ground.

Daniel turned to his right. Sarah stood with the gun aimed at the place the man had fallen. Callum approached with his rifle pointed at the brothers. Daniel removed Silus's gun from his hand and picked up Jasper's. He passed a pistol to Callum and checked to see if Sarah had killed the man. He nodded to Callum who kept his rifle focused on the men. "He's alive."

He ran to Sarah and peeled the gun out of her hand.

"Did they do anything to you?" He examined her face. A bruise formed around her eye. "Son of a bitch. What did they do?"

"Jasper said it was for me kicking him. They didn't do anything else to me," she said in a soft voice. "Did I kill him?"

"No. He's still breathing." He smoothed her hair. "Although he deserves to die, and if I could, I'd kill him."

She wiped her eyes. "He planned to kill you and take me with them."

"I know." Her body trembled, he put his arm around her waist and held her close.

Sheriff Hanson and a deputy thundered toward the cabin on horseback. They dismounted and the sheriff wasted no time placing handcuffs on Silus. The deputy checked the injuries to Jasper and with Callum and Daniel's help laid the unconscious man over one of the horses. Hanson approached Sarah. "I'll need you to come to town and tell your story. I want to see them incarcerated for a long time." He addressed his deputy. "Take the hurt man to Doc Sullivan. I'll lock Silus in the jail."

"We'll follow you back." Daniel led her to where they left the horses. "You were very brave."

"I shot a man." She put her head in her hands and cried.

He pulled her in his arms. "You saved my life. You saved Callum's life, and most important you saved your life. Whether he lives or dies you mustn't feel bad." He wiped a tear from her face. "Boy, am I glad I taught you how to shoot."

She rested her head on his shoulder and hiccupped.

"I'm glad you gave me a gun."

He helped her on the saddle and brushed his hand over the red whelp on her wrist. "How did you free yourself?"

She pulled the scissors from her pocket. "Embroidery shears. I've kept them close for protection since I arrived in Wylder."

He mounted behind her. "Smart girl."

Sarah was tough. None of the girls from back home would do what she did. Travel to a strange place, alone, make a living at whatever she could scrap together. Shoot a man and save another. To say he was proud of her was an understatement. She was the most capable woman he'd ever known, and he loved her.

The party arrived at the sheriff's office. Daniel passed his girl to Callum. "Hold on to her, she may faint." She slid off the horse into the Scotsman's arms, he dismounted and carried her in the building.

Callum fetched Leona and brought her to the Sheriff's office.

Daniel sat and listened while the women told their story. For the first time, he recognized Leona Fabray as a beautiful girl. When she told how they kidnapped Sarah and if she had a gun, she'd have shot them both, she paced around the office until Hanson told her to sit. He enjoyed her animated show and scolded himself for treating the wash woman like she was a second-class citizen. Sarah sat quietly with her hands in her lap as if she were at a social with friends. It would take time for her to recover from this and he prayed she'd stay and not run home. She fled to Wylder because of a tragedy, how would she escape this one?

After the interrogation, Daniel escorted Sarah to

the dress shop. By now the entire town gossiped about what happened.

Widow Lowery fluttered around the shop, taking care of her as if she were her daughter. "Those no-goods. Don't concern yourself. He deserved to be shot. It was either them or you. Winnie would never have forgiven me if anything happened to her only child." She sat her niece in a chair and spouted orders. "Leona, get Doc Sullivan, Daniel, help me get her to her room."

He lifted Sarah into his arms and carried her up the stairs. He wanted to take her to his house, but he'd see what the doctor advised. He placed her on the bed and stood over her. She appeared so tiny even in the little bed. For the first time, he acknowledged the room for what it was. How different this must be from her home. Her trunk was open with clothes draped to keep the wrinkles out. Her embroidery lay on the very top. A basket full of thread and tools sat nearby. A lone kerosene lamp, small pitcher and bowl, and brush and comb competed for space on the table. The jail cell at the sheriff's office was bigger than this. What a remarkable woman. He would love her the rest of his life. He would love her more than she could ever love him.

Doc Sullivan walked in her room without knocking and placed his bag on the table. "Everyone out."

He stood with Widow Lowery on the stoop and waited. He wanted to blame the old woman who seemed more interested in the money she received for board than the safety of her own flesh and blood. But she was just a woman, alone trying to make a living and get by. No, this was his fault. Since Sarah had known him, they'd been robbed and now she could have been killed or God forbid, raped, then killed.

The widow put her hand on his arm. "Thank you for teaching my niece how to shoot, it saved her life." She pulled a handkerchief from her pocket and wiped her eyes. "Sarah doesn't belong here, and I told my sister. They have no idea the perils of the west. Live in their cozy big house, my brother-in-law with his fancy bank job. An adventure, Winnie said, my daughter needs an adventure. I know my sister; she didn't want anything to scar her flawless image. Always did care more for what others thought."

Daniel turned to the dress maker. "I think Sarah has more of you in her than her mother. She's strong and brave. That's what saved her life."

She gave him a smile. "You're a good man. Always thought highly of you, Callum, too. I hope Sarah stays. With you."

He stared at the first grin he'd ever seen from the old woman. "Me, too."

Doc Sullivan allowed them entrance. "She's in a bit of shock, she'll have a black eye, but it'll heal. I put ointment on her wrist for the rope burns. Gave her a powder to help her sleep. The bruises will last a while, but the shock should dissipate in a few days."

He walked Doc Sullivan out. "I'll take care of the bill."

"Right." The doctor turned. "Call me if you need me."

Daniel pulled the chair next to the bed and sat. "I'm staying tonight."

Widow Lowery stood at the foot of the bed. "I'll bring up some coffee later."

Chapter Twenty

Sarah woke to the sound of large pelts of rain hitting her small window. She opened one eye but the left one wouldn't open. She touched the corner of her eye to clear out any crusty remains of sleep but there weren't any. She concentrated and was able to open it a sliver. She turned over to swing her legs off the bed. Daniel sat in a chair, his eyes closed and his head askew as if searching for support. She rose softly and found her mirror. She looked deformed and the swollen skin around her eye took on a blue hue. The events of yesterday raced through her mind. She worried she'd killed Jasper and they would arrest her for murder. Would the court recognize she acted in self-defense for herself, Daniel, and Callum? They had kidnapped her, after all, not the other way around. She poured some water in her glass and drank it. She had her money hidden. She could take it and escape to Savannah before they arrested her. After shooting a man, the scandal seemed like a fairytale. Let them talk about her—at least she'd be safe.

Daniel jerked awake and stood. He took two steps and pulled Sarah in his arms, stroking her hair. "I thought I lost you." He put her face between his hands and examined her injury. "Is it painful?"

"It hurts a bit." She turned her head away from him and stared at the back wall. "I'm ashamed for you to see me. I look ugly."

He put his finger under her chin and turned her head to face him. "Sweetheart, you are beautiful. You'll have a bruise for a couple of weeks, but the swelling will go down soon." He kissed her forehead. "I am so proud of you. You didn't play the victim, you fought back with your ingenuity and bravery. I don't know any woman who would have stood up to Jasper Nelson, not once but twice."

"What if I killed him? Will they put me in jail?" She fell into his embrace and let his warmth soothe her.

"No, sweetheart. They kidnapped you. You defended yourself and me." He smoothed her hair behind her ear, his hand lingered in the soft curls.

"Is that the lawyer talking or my suitor?" She leaned back and searched his eyes for the truth.

"The lawyer says there's enough evidence and witnesses to put the Nelson brothers behind bars for the rest of their lives. The suitor is so proud of his girl and grateful she saved his life." He guided her to the chair. "Doc Sullivan wants to know how you are this morning. I'm going to see him, pay for his visit yesterday and see if he wants to examine you today. How shall I tell him you're faring?"

"Tell him I'm doing better but I want him to check out my eye. I feel like the one-eyed pirates I read about in my novels. The ones who used Savannah as their port of call." She stood and gazed out the window.

"I'll bring you something to eat, you must be starved." He grabbed his gun belt, secured it around his waist, and settled the Stetson on his head.

"I'll take one of Jake's biscuits. Tell him I'll be back to work as soon as I can if he doesn't mind how I look." She stood in the middle of the room not wanting him to leave her.

He placed a quick kiss on her lips. "I'll be back soon."

She held on to the windowsill and stared from the window. The rain soaked the town in a steady drizzle. He hurried down the stairs and crossed Wylder Street to Doc Sullivan's office. Her chest ached in fear that Jasper died from his wound. She gathered clean clothes and descended the stairs clutching the rail with her free hand. The dress shop was empty of customers and she stumbled to the nearest chair, exhausted from the trek from her room.

Widow Lowery walked from the back. "You shouldn't be out of bed; you need to rest."

Desperate to get the filth off her body she demanded. "I need a bath."

Her aunt examined her bruised face. "That piece of manure. Too bad you didn't kill him."

Sarah touched her cheek and winced from the tenderness. "It looks worse than it is. Is Leona around? I smell like a skunk."

"She hasn't been able to do much work because of the rain this morning." The old woman hurried to the back. "Leona, Sarah needs a bath, get the tub ready."

The wash woman rushed from her room and ran straight to her friend. She fell on her knees and put her head in Sarah's lap. "It's my fault, I should have done something to keep them from taking you."

Sarah pulled Leona up and gazed into the eyes of the pretty girl. "You taught me so much. I'm alive because of you."

"But I wasn't there." She shook her head.

"I remembered your advice, look them in the eye. Don't let them know you're scared. Stand up for yourself 'cause no one else will. Also, I had my embroidery scissors and derringer with me." Her knees wobbled as she stood.

Leona gathered her in her arms and hugged her. "I'm so glad you're alive."

Sarah returned the hug, grateful for her sweet friend. She acknowledged her aunt. "Thanks, Aunt Millie for your care of me."

Her aunt nodded and returned a toothy grin. Sarah giggled at the sight and wondered if anyone in town had ever seen the woman smile.

Leona readied her bath while Sarah removed her dirty clothes and piled them in the corner. "Would you mind washing my clothes? I'll pay you."

The girl gathered the dirty linen. "You ain't paying me. I'll take care of 'em."

Sarah put a drop of lilac oil in the water and stepped into the tub.

Leona dropped the clothes in a chair. "Let me help you. Your legs are still weak."

She scooted as far as she could in the little tub letting the warm water soothe the sore muscles in her neck. She rolled her head around until she felt a release.

The wash woman handed her a hot cloth. "Widow says to hold this on your eye until it cools. It'll help the swelling."

She sat in the small tub until her legs cramped and the water cooled. The bath cleansed her body of the dirt and grime and smell of sour whiskey and men's perspiration that clung to her from Jasper's embrace. The familiar lilac scent and the relaxation helped erase some of the bad memories left by the brothers. Would she ever get their faces out of her mind? She put her hands on the side of the tub and pulled herself up.

Leona handed her a large drying cloth and extended her hand. "Easy, don't slip."

With her friend's assistance, she stepped on the rug beside the tub. She stood like a child while Leona dressed her.

The wash woman sat Sarah in a chair and brushed her hair. "You'll get yourself back soon. Don't worry about those two scalawags, they ain't worth it."

She agreed but she'd breathe easier if she found out if Jasper lived and he and Silus were in prison far away from her. What if they escaped? She would be dead. "I've got to go home." Sarah jumped from her chair and paced the room. Her father would protect her, she'd be safe in Savannah, they'd never find her there. She'd take a stage to Denver and board the train home.

Leona put the brush down and grabbed Sarah's arm. "You're as jumpy as a cat. I'll help you back up the stairs." She put her arm around her friend's waist and steadied her.

"No, I need to go back home to my parents. I'm not safe here." She gazed from the back window to the washing area where the washerwoman worked. A foggy haze had settled after the rain.

"I don't see how you can 'til you get better. Come on, I'll get you to your room." Leona held her arm and led her through the store. "Taking Sarah back upstairs. Rain's stopped; I'll get to the washing next." She announced to Mildred.

Widow Lowery peered up from her mending. "I'll check on you after a while."

Sarah stopped and gazed from one side of the street to the other then searched left and right. A few people waded around mud and puddles of water.

Leona put Sarah's arm around her shoulder and shuffled her up the stairs. "You hungry?"

"Daniel's getting me something." She leaned against the wall as she placed the key in the lock and turned. "You better get to work before Widow Lowery fires you."

"She ain't gonna but I got enough work for two days, better get to it." Leona stood at the top of the stairs. "You know where I am if ya need me."

Sarah rearranged her belongings in the trunk to make room for the dresses and hats she'd purchased in Wylder. She could pack everything she owned in it and return home. The last few days proved she wasn't cut out for this kind of life. She turned to collect her gloves from the table and the picture of Daniel halted her work.

Their day in the city had been so much fun until they were robbed at gunpoint. Maybe she could convince him to sell his ranch and move to Savannah. They could live a civilized life together. He could open a law office and she would have her friends over for afternoon tea. She pictured him in a suit sitting behind a large desk reading legal papers. The picture in her mind faded, he wasn't her Daniel. He thrived on the land, his long hair flowing behind him as he rode Kentucky, or his take-charge stance when he commanded his team of horses in his wagon. She admired the way his sidearm rested on his thigh, reminded her of a gunslinger. Daniel might be from the East, but he belonged to Wyoming.

A knock sounded. Her frazzled nerves sent a shock through her. She peered out the window, relieved to see Daniel. Sarah glanced in the mirror, smoothed her hair, and opened the door. "Come in."

He stepped inside. "Jake sent you a plate. I told him you only wanted a biscuit, but he insisted."

She sat in the chair, he placed the plate on her lap, and she peeked under the napkin. A huge biscuit dripping in butter set atop scrambled eggs, fried potatoes, and bacon. She inhaled the scent, her stomach growled loud enough for Daniel to hear. Embarrassed she reached for the fork. "Sorry, guess I'm hungrier than I thought."

He placed the Stetson on the table and sat on the bed. "Eat as much as you can, you need the strength. Doc Sullivan says he'll come by this afternoon."

She ate a few bites but her ravenous stomach demanded all of it. She devoured the entire plate of food and sopped the grease with the remainder of the bread. "Jake makes a good breakfast."

He poured some water into a glass, passed it to her and took the plate. "He said to tell you to take as much time as you need. Your job is waiting when you recover."

She drank a sip of water. "What about Jasper?"

"Doc Sullivan said he's too mean to die. Already got him in the jail. Sheriff Hanson worried as he got stronger, he'd try to escape. Soon as he recuperates, both will be sent to Cheyenne to await trial." He nodded toward her trunk. "Going somewhere?"

Yes, she wanted to scream. *I'm going to leave this godforsaken place and go home*. She gazed in his dark eyes, the brown seemed black today and they were red where he hadn't slept. She couldn't do it, he loved her, he'd already told her. How could she leave him? But how could she stay? "Just straightening up. If I must remain in this room 'til I'm better, I don't want to live in a pigsty."

He fell to his knees in front of her chair and took both of her hands in his. "I wouldn't blame you if you left. I know you could never make Wylder your home."

She pulled him close and rested her head on his shoulder. The smell of leather and Daniel washed over her. The terror of this place dissipated when he held her. "I can't talk about this now."

He scooped her in his arms and deposited her on the small bed. "Rest. The doc will be by soon to examine your eye."

She settled against the mattress. "What are you going to do?"

He sat in the chair. "Sit right here and watch you."

Chapter Twenty-One

Daniel held the reins tight. Kentucky sensed the direction they headed and galloped faster the closer they came to the ranch. "Calm down, boy. You'll be in your stall soon." It had been days since he slept in a bed. He'd boarded Kentucky at the livery. He liked Chet Daniels, but he trusted no one with his woman or his horse. Sarah's injuries improved, Widow Lowery and Leona promised they would watch over her. The Nelson brothers were in jail and since Sarah had shot Jasper, he figured no one else in town would mess with her again. That image brought a chuckle. The familiar arch welcomed him home and Kentucky trotted straight to the barn without guidance.

Callum met him and held the reins while he dismounted. "Everything all right?"

"Aye, be fine." Callum led Kentucky to his stall. "How is the lass?"

"She's better. Face still swollen but she's getting stronger. Talking about going back to work." He grabbed a bucket of oats and the curry comb to care for his horse.

"I got this." Callum removed the saddle pad. "Ye look like yer sleepwalking. There's food in the kitchen. Eat and sleep, that's what ye need."

Daniel draped the saddlebag over his shoulder. "Thanks, Red." He ambled toward his house. He hadn't been this tired on their long journey to Wyoming in the wagon. He deposited the money in the safe and moseyed toward the kitchen. Callum had made an apple pie and left some biscuits and jerky wrapped in a napkin. He devoured the food and drank water. A bowl of apples sat on the counter and he ate one while he pondered what Sarah would do. He'd seen the trunk neatly packed. He accepted the fact when he made his decision to court her, she'd likely leave first chance she got. He loved her more than his life but would love be enough to make her stay? His footsteps echoed through the empty house as he made his way to the office. He poured a finger of spirits and downed it. He welcomed the burn and poured another. The good whiskey soothed his fretfulness. He tugged off his boots and reclined on the settee. Memories of Sarah naked and willing in his bed kept him downstairs. He couldn't sleep in his bed, not with the memories he had of their time together. Not with her alone and hurting in her small bed. Not with knowing she'd soon leave.

He woke before dawn, his back ached from sleeping in the small space. He stretched and walked to the window. The sky was clear, and the sun beamed through the curtains, animals needed attention and his stomach growled. On his way to the hen house to gather eggs for breakfast he found Callum emptying a bucket of feed for the cow. "Had breakfast?"

The Scotsman placed the pail on the ground. "No, doing chores first."

"Come to the house when you're done. I'll have us some eggs and salt pork. Still got some of those catheads left." He made his way to the hen house.

Daniel and Callum feasted on scrambled eggs, salt

pork, hard cheese, biscuits, and syrup. Daniel poured more coffee into his friend's cup. "What have I missed?"

"The pregnant mare had her foal. She's a fine little filly." He cut open a biscuit and filled it with cheese.

"Any problems? I should have been here to help." Daniel pushed his plate away and rested his elbows on the table.

"Easy birth. This wasn't her first, the girl knew what to do." He put his hands on the table and leaned forward. "What's bothering ye?"

His chest tightened and his right hand balled into a fist. He gathered the strength to admit the truth. "Sarah's leaving." He croaked the response not recognizing his own voice.

"Did she tell you in her own words?" Callum crossed his arms. "Could be you want her to…"

Before Callum could finish his sentence, Daniel jumped up. His chair tumbled on its side and he stepped over it. "I don't want her to go."

Callum crossed his hands over his chest. "Did ye tell her ye want her to stay? Did ye propose marriage? Did ye tell her ye can't live without her?"

The urge to punch a hole in the wall caused the fingers in his right hand to flex and stiffen. "I told her I loved her."

"Aye, did she tell you back?" He scooted his chair from the table.

Daniel turned and glared at his friend. "No, she didn't."

"Women want to be pursued." The Scotsman poured more coffee into both their cups. "Sit."

Daniel righted the chair. "I don't need your

advice." He sat and held his cup.

"I think ye do." He gave his friend a smile. "Ye know why the others left? It wasn't because they didn't like this town, or they wanted to search for their treasure. Those were excuses. They left because you didn't love them enough."

He glared at Red, the words his friend spoke were a fist to his gut. "And you think Sarah will stay because I told her I loved her?"

"No, I think Sarah will remember how you looked at her the first day you met her. How you were ready to take a bullet for her and how she shot a man to protect you. Those three words can be said millions of times a day. It's the acts of love that make it real." He stood and put his plate in the sink. "Give the lass time." He turned to go. "Got work to do."

He conceded, Callum told the truth. He believed he loved Becca and the others, but he'd give up all the times he spent with them for one hour with Sarah.

****

Daniel stood at the stall and watched the filly drink her fill of the mare's milk. The foal had a cinnamon-colored coat and the same white marking on her forehead as the mare. The scene reminded him how precious life is. The sound Jasper's pistol made when the kidnapper cocked it and pointed it at his head would remain in his ears a long time. When the shot rang out, he waited for the bullet to hit him. In the same moment Jasper hit the floor he spotted Sarah; her eyes held a determined self-control.

He sashayed out of the barn with Kentucky saddled and ready to go. "Going to town," he said to Callum.

His friend brushed Icefall's coat. "That's where

you need to be. I'll take care of things."

****

Daniel hurried up the stairs to Sarah's room. She welcomed him in. He examined the injury on her face and eye. The swelling had gone down but her eye was black and blue from the bruise. He enveloped her in his arms. "I missed you."

"I missed you," she whispered. "Kiss me."

He brushed her lips with his, not wanting to cause her any pain.

She put her arms around his neck. "I'm not going to break. Kiss me like you mean it."

His mouth took hers tasting and testing how far he could go without hurting her. She pulled the leather strap out of his hair. He stopped kissing and turned his head from side to side to free the ponytail.

She ran her hands through his hair and presented him with a demanding kiss, her tongue exploring his mouth. "I love kissing you." She sighed.

Her brazen move fanned the flames and his body thrummed with desire. His hand drifted to her breast; he ran his thumb over the pebble hard peak. It was too soon. She was broken and afraid but damn he wanted inside her now. As if she read his mind, she stood and led him to the bed. "Sarah, no, you're still recovering."

She held both his hands. "I need you. I need to know I'm all right. I need to know you love me."

He kissed her as if their very lives depended on the connection.

She stepped out of her bloomers and unfastened the closure of his pants. "Please." She took him in her hand.

The touch of her hands on him knocked the breath

out of his lungs. He pushed her to the bed and entered her. The sweet essence of Sarah surrounded him. The lovemaking was frenzied, both bodies desperate for the coupling. He poured his soul into her as she moaned and called his name. He withdrew from her. "I didn't hurt you, did I?"

She put her hands on his face. "You didn't hurt me."

He gathered her in his arms and let her body slide out of his embrace to stand before him. "I'll help you dress."

"Doc Sullivan says I'm doing fine, and I can go back to work." She stepped into her bloomers.

Laying on the bed naked with her in his arms for the afternoon wasn't an option. Widow Lowery or Leona could come up the stairs any minute to check on her. He stepped into his pants. The beginning of embroidery on a dress sat in the basket. "Working on something?" He fastened his buttons.

"Yes, a dress for Miss Adelaide. I'm going back to work for Jake tomorrow." She poured water into a glass for him.

"Then what?" He searched her eyes for a hint.

She stepped toward him and put a hand on his chest. "Not sure what you mean."

He put his hand under her chin and turned it up. "After what you've been through, I figured you'd be on the next train out of Wylder."

She crossed her hands over her chest and walked toward the window. "I've been struggling with the decision."

He pulled her in his arms, her back to his chest. "I wouldn't blame you. Wylder's no place for a fine woman." He kissed the top of her head. "I love you and I want what's best for you." He ground out the words in a whisper.

She turned and pulled his face to hers. "I don't want to talk about this." She kissed his lips.

He kissed her as if he'd never do it again.

Chapter Twenty-Two

Sarah stirred a large bowl of cornbread mixture while Jake poured hot bacon grease into the batter. "Cornbread is easy to make."

"All cooking is simple if you know what you're doing." He positioned two heavy iron skillets on top of the stove. "Pour the batter in equal portions into the hot pans. If you get your pan hot and have enough grease in it, the bread won't stick."

The bell on the front door sounded. "I'll see who came in." She scraped all the mix out of the bowl and rinsed it with water before going to the dining room.

"Tell 'em lunch'll be ready in about thirty." Jake put the skillets in the oven.

She entered the dining room. A man stood staring out at the street. The gentleman appeared out of place wearing a long coat and top hat. She hadn't seen a top hat since she left Savannah. "Lunch won't be ready for thirty minutes but you can sit and wait. I'll bring you some coffee."

The man turned to face her. "So you're a servant now?"

She bounced two steps and landed in her father's arms. "Papa." The brave face she'd put on since the attack faded. The dam burst and the tears flowed like the river she loved and missed. He held her and she sobbed, unable to stop until all emotions she'd held close were spent.

Sarah wiped her face with the handkerchief he offered and motioned to a table. "Have a seat. How's Mother, is she here? When did you arrive?"

He pulled out a chair. "Your mother is in Savannah." He placed his hat on the table. "Millie sent us a telegram. I came to take you home." He put two fingers under her chin and examined her face. "You still have a bruise, but I don't think you'll have any lasting damage to your face."

Home, the place she'd longed for since her first encounter with the bad men on the day she arrived. The place she wanted to run to after she shot Jasper. The only place on earth she felt safe. "What's the talk in Savannah?" she ventured to ask her father.

"There will always be gossip, girl." He grunted under his breath. "If Winifred had listened to me and ignored the biddies you wouldn't be in this predicament. I take full responsibility for what happened. I have tickets for us on the next train back."

She placed her hand on his arm. "I can't just up and leave. I have work to do. Jake needs me and I have a dress I'm working on for Miss Willowby." She walked to the window and stared at her little room over the store.

He stood and took his hat from the table. "Daughter, I've come all this way worried about your welfare. Millie said you were kidnapped and shot a man. The evidence of his beating is still on your face. You should be happy to see me and know I care and want you to come home."

"What about Mother?" Sarah asked.

"Winnie is just as concerned as I." He stood beside

her.

"Is she, Papa?" She turned to face her father, the answer plain on his face. "Mama's the reason I'm in this town."

He positioned his hat on his head. "You have a few days to get your business done."

She hugged her arms around her chest and stared until he rounded the corner then she took off running. "Wait, where are you staying?"

He halted and turned to face her. "I'm at the Vincent House Hotel."

Sarah went back to her safe place, the cafe. She'd cleaned every spot of the restaurant, scrubbed the floor on her knees, served everyone in the town of Wylder and learned to cook in the kitchen. This job had made her a responsible woman, for the experience she would always be grateful. Papa who'd only traveled to border states with Georgia had traveled all the way to Wyoming to see her safely home. She'd craved his love and approval all her life. If she didn't go back with him, he'd be heartbroken. She wiped off every table as she gathered her wits about her.

Jake came out of the kitchen, wiping his hands on his apron. "Cornbread's ready. They decide not to wait?"

She sat at a table dividing knives, forks, and spoons into a tray. A lump formed in her throat. "My father, he just arrived in Wylder. He came to take me home."

"Did he now?" Her boss pulled up a chair and sat. "How you feel 'bout that?"

She found a soiled spoon and set it aside. Her mind raced searching for answers. "I've been homesick and longing for home since I arrived."

"I hope you can sound more convincing if you're asked to testify against Jasper and Silus." He walked in the kitchen.

She sat in a chair and put her head in her hands. She could blame her reluctance to leave on her job, Miss Adelaide's work and even her friendship with Leona. The biggest qualm was the realization of not seeing Daniel. It caused a physical ache worse than when Jasper hit her. She exhaled a deep breath and went back to the kitchen to assist Jake.

The bell on the door rang incessantly signaling the rush of the afternoon meal. She welcomed the distraction as she chatted and served the friends she'd come to look forward to waiting on day to day. She'd taken their good-natured ribbing about shooting one of the most notorious bad men ever to call Wylder home. Every man and woman congratulated her on ridding the community of the brothers Nelson.

Sarah rushed through her duties after the patrons left the restaurant. She'd missed her Papa most of all and wanted to spend time with him. She said goodbye to Jake and hurried to the hotel. "Can you tell me what room Mr. John Miller is in?" The young man looked her over as he studied the register. "He's my father. He's from Savannah, Georgia. He told me he had a room in this hotel."

"Upstairs, room two zero six." The man said as he closed the book.

She hurried to his room and knocked.

"Who is it?" He called through the door.

"It's me," she said as she turned the knob. The key clicked in the lock. She stood face to face with her father. "Did you have lunch? I hoped you'd come back to Jake's Place and eat. He serves good food."

"I ate in the hotel dining room. It was passable." He stood at the window.

The lace curtains caught her eye. The sun beamed into the room and she could see dust swirling in the air even though the entire place was spotless. She gazed around the large room. It held a good size bed, chest, desk, chair, and washstand. It was decorated in blue, white and yellow. "This is a beautiful room. I've been told this is the best hotel in town."

"Mildred recommended it." He got his coat and put his hat on. "Want to show me the town. I need a walk about."

"Sure." She strolled with him down the wide stairs to the first floor. They exited the hotel and turned right. "I'll show you the bank first."

They entered Goldmount Bank and stood to the side of the entrance. "It's not as big as our bank in Savannah." She said as she waved to the bank teller.

The owner came out of his office and approached her father. "Mr. Frederick Mountroy, is there anything I can help you with?"

Her father shook the man's outstretched hand. "Mr. John Miller, I'm President of Savannah Bank and Trust, Savannah, Georgia. My daughter is showing me the town. Nice place you have."

"Pleasure to meet another banker. I'm from back east myself, Knoxville, Tennessee." He motioned toward his office. "Care to sit and visit?"

He shook his head. "Not today, going to spend time with my daughter. I'll come back another time, see how you operate in the west."

"Of course." He stepped aside and let them exit.

They waited while two buggies and one wagon went by before crossing Wylder Street. "The apothecary is nice if you need any medicine and the bakery has small cakes as good as Savannah." Sarah led her father toward Buckboard Alley. They crossed and sauntered by the mercantile. "Finn Wylder owns the store. He has some nice things if you want to take something home to Mama."

"I'll come back another day. Show me where you've been living." He held her arm and guided her down the walk.

"Didn't Widow Lowery tell you?" They rounded the corner at Sidewinder Lane.

He stopped and stared. "Widow Lowery?"

"People in town know her as Widow Lowery." She started up the stairs. "I live above the dress shop."

She unlocked the door. "It's small but it's enough room for me." She transferred the basket of embroidery from the bed to the floor.

He gazed around the room. "Winnie told me you would stay with Mildred and I imagined you'd have a nice room with amenities, not a space the size of your mother's dressing room."

"It's big enough for me and the board is cheaper than Culpepper's Boarding House." She sat on the bed. "Have a seat in the chair."

He crossed his arms over his chest and bellowed. "Your aunt is charging you board."

"Papa." She placed her hand on his arm. "Don't blame Aunt Mildred. This is a different place than Savannah. Everyone works hard to make a living. I thought she was being cruel, making me stay in this room and forcing me to get a job to pay my way. I've learned more from my experiences than I ever would in Savannah. I know what being responsible for oneself is and I'm grateful for the lesson."

He gazed around the room. "Get your things, I'll get you a room at the Vincent."

"No." She gestured around the small space. "I'm content in my room. I'll stay until we leave for home."

A knock sounded and Daniel's voice rang out. "Sweetheart, are you home?"

John Miller opened the door. "Who are you?"

He put his hand on his revolver. "I'm Daniel Taylor, who are you?"

Sarah positioned herself between them. "Papa, this is Daniel, he's a friend of mine."

Mr. Miller pushed his daughter aside and stared eyeball to eyeball with the younger man. "You're the cause of my daughter's kidnapping. They wanted to extort money from you and kidnapped my daughter for leverage. You have a lot of nerve coming here."

Sarah tugged her father's hand and pulled him away from Daniel. "Papa, he's my beau."

Her father roared. "Daughter, you fled to the west to escape a scandal and now you've taken up with some cowboy."

Sarah moved to stand beside Daniel. Where was Papa and her mother when she needed them? They encouraged her to travel to the west for their benefit not hers. If not for Daniel she'd be dead and buried in the Wylder cemetery. She gazed at the man who had taken care of her since she departed the train on the hot summer day.

He gazed at her and turned his attention to her father. "Mr. Miller, let's start all over. My name is

Daniel Taylor and I'm a rancher. I raise quarter horses and live just outside town."

"I don't care if you're the mayor. It's not proper for a man to call on a single helpless woman, alone in a strange town." He drank from the glass of water Sarah passed him.

She led him to the chair. "Papa, sit before your heart gives out."

Daniel sat on the bed and faced Sarah's father.

She sat beside her beau and reached for her father's hand. "Daniel saved my life twice. The day I arrived the Nelson brothers harassed me on the way from the train station to the dress shop. He fought them to protect me. When they got their chance, they kidnapped me, and the money was a bonus. Their plan was to kill Daniel when he gave them the cash and take me with them."

"Had I known all this, you would have been back to Savannah on the next train. I'll never forgive Mildred for the way she's treated you. And you, son." He scowled at Daniel. "I appreciate you rescuing my daughter but if you are the gentleman you say, you would have placed her on the next train back home to her family."

Sarah interrupted, taking full responsibility. "It was my choice, Papa. No one held a gun to my head and made me stay. Mama's the reason I came, yet you blame me for everything."

Mr. Miller pierced her with a stare. "Girl, you will not speak bad of your mother. I admit she had a hand in this fiasco, and I'll tend to the matter on my return."

"I have a suggestion. Let's continue this discussion at the Vincent House Restaurant." Daniel stood and walked toward the door. "I believe we all need some fresh air."

Daniel's idea proved a welcome distraction from her little room cramped with the three of them arguing. The sun faded and the air fell into a comfortable temperature. The walk created a lighter mood as they entered the building.

Daniel left them and approached the hotel manager. "Dinner for three, please."

Sarah put her arm through her father's and whispered. "He's really a nice man."

He stared at his daughter, shook his head, and let out a long breath.

The trepidation of having dinner with her father and the man she loved melted to contentment as little-by-little Daniel won over her father with his intelligence and quick wit. Sarah observed the transformation and learned the art of listening and showing bona fide interest in another's views. Daniel would make a great lawyer if he decided to give up ranching. He'd have to cut his hair and wear a suit. She sipped hot tea and pondered the image. Her mind slipped to how he looked in his underwear when her father asked her a question.

"What do you think?" He drank a sip of wine.

Sarah's face heated and Daniel gave her a smile as if he read her mind. She remembered hearing something about banks. "Well, Papa, things are different in the west. If Daniel lived in Savannah, I know he'd trust all his money to your bank."

"Exactly." He motioned the waiter over. "My check please."

"Mr. Taylor has taken care of the bill, sir." He bent over slightly at the waist.

John nodded toward Daniel. "Thank you for dinner."

"You are very welcome. I want you and Sarah to visit my ranch and I'll show you some of the beautiful Wyoming countryside." He placed his napkin beside his empty plate. "I'll pick you up at ten in the morning."

He turned his attention to his daughter. She nodded. "Ten in the morning it is."

Daniel stood and pulled out Sarah's chair. "I'll see your daughter safely back."

John Miller stopped at the bottom of the stairs and extended his hand. "Enjoyed meeting you."

"The pleasure was all mine." Daniel returned the handshake.

"See you in the morning, Papa." Sarah tiptoed and placed a kiss on her father's cheek.

The evening air was cool, and she walked close to Daniel to keep the chill off her shoulders. "Thank you for being so nice to my father. I don't know how to handle him."

"Seems all I do is rescue you from men." He put his arm around her waist and led her across the street.

They ascended the stairs. He gave her a quick kiss before she entered her small apartment. "See you in the morning. Be sure and lock up."

She entered, turned the key, and placed the chair under the knob. She peered from the window as her love disappeared through the streets of Wylder. The pang that hit her stomach hurt as bad as the blow Jasper made to her face. Daniel and the times he made love to her in this room flashed through her memory.

She had a choice to make and from the failed decisiveness in her past she struggled with her options.

Chapter Twenty-Three

Daniel rose before sunrise to prepare for his day with Mr. Miller and Sarah. He lit several kerosene lamps in his office to see the dust that had collected over the last month. Spending time with Sarah had been his priority, not keeping a spotless house. He placed the important papers in the top drawer of his desk and stacked newspapers in a neat bundle. After an inspection of all the rooms he hurried upstairs to clean himself and dress in respectable clothes. Mr. Miller's attire was that of a refined man. Something he wasn't, but he had some decent clothes from his time in law school that would suit the occasion. He tied his hair with the leather strap and walked to the barn.

Callum readied the two-horse buggy rubbing the seats with a damp cloth. "Top of the mornin' to ye."

"Morning." Daniel walked past him to one of the waiting horses. "Appreciate you cooking food for us today." He guided the horse to the front of the carriage.

Callum helped with the other animal. "I'll be serving stovies. Made shortbread yesterday. It be no trouble at all." They worked in tandem securing the horses.

"You make a good stew. Mutton or beef?" He pulled a bit of hay out of the horse's mane.

"Mutton. Made a special trip to the sheep ranch this morning. Stovies is cooking as we speak." He stood to the side.

Daniel climbed in the seat. "See you in a few hours. Going to show Mr. Miller some of the countryside."

He parked his buggy in front of the Vincent House Hotel and wandered inside. Sarah and her father lounged in the front sitting room. John Miller read a newspaper and she worried her hands. He entered the room and presented her with a smile.

She returned the smile, stood, adjusted her gloves, and put her drawstring bag on her arm. "We're ready."

Mr. Miller put his paper down and stood. He extended his hand. "Mr. Taylor."

"No need to be formal, call me Daniel." He shook the older man's hand.

He guided the carriage toward his favorite spot, the creek he'd taken Sarah on their first date. He parked the buggy and assisted her from her seat. With the reins secured to a tree he led them to the water's edge. "Wanted to show you how the mountains rise in the distance above the treetops."

"This is beautiful land." Mr. Miller studied the scenery. "Georgia has pretty mountains in the north of the state. You get a lot of snow here?"

Daniel stared at the highest peak. "We do and the picture nature paints on the ridge rivals no other."

"You have a rough life." He addressed the young man.

"Yes." Images of his Kentucky home sparked his memory. "But you know sir, I wouldn't trade this lifestyle for my easy life back east."

He turned the carriage onto his land proud to show off what he'd worked on for nigh five years.

"Lex Taylor Ranch." Mr. Miller read the signage on the arch.

Daniel parked the buggy in front of his house.

Callum stepped off the porch and took charge of the carriage. "Good morning to ye."

Daniel helped Sarah from her seat and introduced Callum to her father. "Mr. Miller, this is Callum MacPhilip. He's a Scotsman and a good friend. I couldn't have made it to Wyoming or started this ranch without him."

The older man nodded his head but stood back from the pair of horses. "Pleased to make your acquaintance."

Callum tied the reins and extended his hand. "Pleasure be mine."

After the greetings and handshake Daniel led them up the stairs to his wide front porch. "Want to show you my house and then we'll tour the barns." He gave them a guided tour of the upstairs and downstairs. He almost laughed out loud as Sarah made oohs and aahs as if she'd never been in his house before. They walked through the dining room to the kitchen. The table was set with his Wedgewood china and fine silver. Red wine in a crystal carafe ready for pouring sat next to his plate at the head of the table. "Callum has made his special Scottish stew for lunch."

"Yes, I smell the delicious aroma." Mr. Miller said as he gazed around the sunny room. "Beautiful house. Who was the architect?"

He opened the kitchen door and stood back to let them enter. "I designed it after my parents' home in Lexington. Callum and I built everything on the property. Well, most all of it, I hired some hands when we needed them." He poured water from a pitcher and presented glasses to Sarah and her father.

The old man sipped the water and examined the room from floor to ceiling. "Does Callum live with you?"

"No, he has a small cabin further into the land. He likes to be surrounded by trees, says the scenery reminds him of his home country." Daniel opened the back door. "Let's head to the barn."

Chickens raced between them as they walked.

John stepped around a hen pecking on the ground. "You have other animals."

"We're self-sufficient. Chicken, hogs, and a milk cow. Get our beef and mutton from ranchers between here and Cheyenne." He shooed the chickens.

The Scotsman groomed Icefall just outside the barn. Daniel addressed the old man. "Ever seen a Clydesdale?"

"Can't say I have." He stared. "Beautiful specimen."

"He's a gentle giant." Callum led the huge animal to them.

Sarah rubbed his mane and pressed her head to his. "Pet him, Papa; isn't he lovely?"

Mr. Miller came forward and placed his hand on Icefall's head and rubbed. "Certainly is."

"Let me show you the quarter horses." Daniel escorted them to the fenced area where several horses grazed. "My parents raise racehorses in Lexington, but quarter horses bring the most money in the west."

The older gentleman put his hand on the top rail. "Impressive place you've got. Never imagined anything as beautiful as this existed in the world."

"Wyoming is a peaceful place, most of the time." He put his arm on Sarah's back and drew her close. "Let's head to the house for lunch."

She placed her hand in the crook of his elbow and walked beside him.

Daniel seated Sarah to his right and her father to his left. Callum poured wine in each glass and took his seat opposite him. He passed around the Scottish stew. "Hope everyone likes lamb."

Sarah took a biscuit from the silver tray. "I learned how to make biscuits from my boss at the restaurant but mine aren't as good as Callum's."

Her father placed a biscuit on his bread plate. "You'll have to make them when we return to Savannah."

Anger caused heat to flow through Daniel's body and he had trouble swallowing. His fork grew heavy in his hand and he wanted to throw it against the wall but placed it on his plate instead. "When are you going back?" He sent a searing gaze toward his girl. She sipped wine and ignored him. He stared at her until she met his gaze. The sadness in her eyes was his answer. "What day does your train leave?" He addressed the question to the old man.

"Tuesday at noon." He nodded toward his daughter and drank a sip of wine. "It'll be good to have the daughter close, so we don't worry over her."

He struggled to keep the stew from rising from his stomach. He poured more wine in his glass and drank. He peered at Callum and perceived the concern in his friend's face.

He did his best to remain civilized until he delivered his guests back to town. He parked the buggy in front of the hotel. Mr. Miller thanked him for the lunch and the day on the ranch. He shook his hand and wished him a safe trip home.

Sarah stood beside her father. "Daniel, do you mind walking me back to my room? I know Papa's tired and needs to rest."

He ground his teeth. "Of course." He didn't touch her and walked a slight distance from her all the way. He entered her room and removed his Stetson and held it in his hand. "When were you going to tell me?"

She put her reticule on the table. "Daniel, I..."

He pulled her in his arms and kissed her as if she were the last person on earth he would ever kiss. His fingers raked over the satin skin of her neck. He tasted her lips, deepened the kiss, and left his brand on her tongue. The sound of her whimper made him ache for her. To take her one more time would be a memory to warm him on cold nights, but he couldn't. The agony would be too great. He pushed her from him and ran his gaze from the top of her head to her boots and burned the image into the crevasse of his brain.

A tear slid down her face and she wiped it with her gloved hand. "Daniel, I'm sorry. I didn't know Papa would come here and demand that I go home."

He put his finger under her chin and turned her face toward his. She made her decision as he knew she would. Sarah was no different than the others. He refused to say anything that would hurt her and turned to walk down the stairs one last time.

Daniel arrived at the ranch and took care of the buggy and horses. Callum plowed a small plot for their winter greens and waved. He had no desire to talk so he finished his work in the barn and made his way to his house for a large glass of bourbon.

To forget his troubles and the only woman he'd ever loved he refused to eat, bathe or work. When the liquor wore off and the pain started, Daniel took to drinking again until his body numbed, and his mind blurred from the memory of losing her. During lucid times, he glanced out the window to observe Callum go about the business of the ranch. Guilt of neglecting his work had him sitting on the porch nursing a cup of coffee.

The Scotsman approached. "You decide to come back to life?"

"Only because responsibility wills it so." He stared in the distance. "What day is it?"

"Tuesday." Callum stood on the steps.

He had the urge to throw the damn cup on the ground and grab the good whiskey. "What time is it?"

"Eleven in the morn." Callum stepped to the side of the house and drew Kentucky to the porch, saddled and ready to go. "At least go and see her one last time, or was she as unimportant as the rest, not worth yer time?"

Daniel had never wanted to strike another man the way he wanted to punch Red right now. "You son of a bitch, you know nothing about this."

"Aye, I do." He rubbed Kentucky's side.

He examined his appearance and inhaled the smell of his unwashed body. He'd not changed clothes for days and his hair hung around his face uncombed. He pulled the leather cord out of his pocket and secured his hair. "Give me the reins." He propelled the horse to the limit on the road to Wylder and raced through town as people scurried out of his way. Kentucky danced in a circle when he brought the animal to a halt in front of the train station. A whistle blew, and the train chugged away from town. "Of all damn days for the train to be on time," he cursed under his breath. The iron horse headed east with his heart. He lost the one person he'd never get over. He dismounted and led Kentucky to a water trough. "Sorry, buddy. We were too late."

A female voice addressed him. "Daniel Taylor, where's your hat?" Her gaze raked over his body. "And are those the same clothes you wore last I saw you? You look like you slept in the barn with Kentucky."

"But I thought…" His lips quivered near a tear-induced breakdown. He blinked his eyes to make sure he wasn't experiencing a drunk's hallucination.

She strolled toward him. "Papa left on the train, he missed Mother and needed to get back to work. I promised him I'd come home if you said no to marrying me."

He gazed into her eyes; the sun brought out the yellow flecks mingled with the ice blue. He wiped a rouge tear from his cheek. "You'll marry me?"

A big smile filled her face. She tiptoed and presented a soft peck of a kiss on his cheek. "Yes, Daniel Taylor, I will marry you."

Chapter Twenty-Four

Widow Lowery's Dress Shop was quiet for a Saturday morning. The only ladies in the store were the widow, Sarah, and Leona. "How do I look?" Sarah came out of the dressing room, Leona followed behind.

"Turn around." Widow Lowery examined the dress. "Bow isn't right." She untied the ribbon and pulled it tighter. "Want to show off that tiny waist of yours. Won't have it long, though."

"Why not?" She smoothed the white satin skirt.

The old lady smiled at her niece. "I imagine Daniel will have you with child soon. Won't be able to hold on to your tiny figure much longer."

The most wonderful excitement settled in her belly. She touched her aunt's arm. "When it happens, I want you to be a part of the baby's life. Will you promise me?" A tear welled up in the woman's eye. Sarah wanted to hug her aunt, but she knew she'd turn her away just like she did the hot summer day Sarah arrived in Wylder. It seemed like years ago, so much had happened.

Widow Lowery looked away and fiddled with a bolt of fabric. "Just don't think I'm gonna be some caretaker to leave the wild ones with while y'all go off and enjoy yourselves."

Sarah shared a knowing smile with Leona. She hastened to her friend and smoothed the lace on the blue gown. "You are lovely in a dress."

The wash woman brushed her hand away. "Just wearin' this 'cause you asked. Never wanted to dress up, I'm not comfortable."

"Thank you for doing this for me." She gazed out the window of the store. "The carriage is here."

The ladies were helped into their seats by Chet Daniels. He drove the buggy the short distance to Saint Joseph's Episcopal Church. "Fine day for a weddin'."

She smiled at the man and nodded. People came out of the stores and waved.

She was home. In Wylder, Wyoming. And she had no doubt Daniel would be waiting at the altar.

A word about the author...

Jane Lewis is a native of Atlanta and lover of all things Southern. She writes historical romance with strong heroines and happy-ever-after endings. When she isn't writing, she enjoys yoga, weight training, cooking, playing music, and spending time with her real-life hero, her husband.

She is a PAN member of Romance Writers of America and Georgia Romance Writers. She was a 2016 finalist in the Hearts Through History, Post-Victorian/World War II category for her first romance novel, *Love at Five Thousand Feet*.

www.janelewisauthor.com

Thank you for purchasing
this publication of The Wild Rose Press, Inc.

For questions or more information
contact us at
info@thewildrosepress.com.

The Wild Rose Press, Inc.
www.thewildrosepress.com

CPSIA information can be obtained
at www.ICGtesting.com
Printed in the USA
FSHW021950300321
80019FS